"THERE IS SOMETHING VERY STRANGE HAPPENING AT THE SYMPHONY. SOMEONE KILLED PETER, AND I BELIEVE THAT MORE DEATHS WILL FOLLOW," THE MAN SAID.

"What makes you think that?" Phoebe asked.

Instead of answering, the man cocked his head suddenly to the side. Phoebe could hear the sound of music dancing faintly on the breeze. Without a word the man turned and stepped into the street. Stunned, Phoebe watched as a truck hit him and sent his body flying through the air.

She screamed and ran toward his body, cars screeching to a halt around her. She reached him, and even as she bent down she knew it was too late. His eyes were already fixed and staring at something she couldn't see.

She slumped down next to the body. *I've lost another Innocent*, she realized. *And I don't even know why.*

More titles in the

All Simon & Schuster books are available by post from:
Simon & Schuster Cash Sales. PO Box 29
Douglas, Isle of Man IM99 1BQ
Credit cards accepted.
Please telephone 01624 677237
fax 01624 670923
Internet http://www.bookpost.co.uk
or email: bookshop@enterprise.net for details

PIED PIPER

An original novel by Debbie Viguié

Based on the hit TV series created by

Constance M. Burge

Simon & Schuster, London

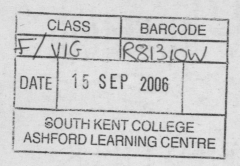
First published in Great Britain in 2004 by Simon & Schuster UK Ltd.
Africa House, 64–78 Kingsway, London WC2B 6AH
A Viacom Company

Originally published in 2004 by Simon Spotlight Entertainment
an imprint of Simon & Schuster Children's Division, New York

A CIP catalogue record for this book is available from the British Library
upon request.

ISBN 0689875339

1 3 5 7 9 10 8 6 4 2

Printed by Cox & Wyman Ltd, Reading, Berkshire

*To my two muses: Richard Reynolds and
Boysen Bear. Without you,
none of this would have been possible.*

Acknowledgments

I need to thank Elizabeth Bracken for being a fabulous editor and really coming through for me when the chips were down. Thanks to Micol Ostow, who also worked with me on this project. Thanks to my mother, Barbara Reynolds, and my husband, Scott Viguié, for all their love and support.

PIED PIPER

Chapter

1

Piper Halliwell groaned and slowly sat up, rubbing her shoulder. It was tender to the touch and she was sure she'd be bruised in the morning. "I hate when that happens," she said, shaking her head to clear it. "Did we vanquish him?" she asked, glancing toward the spot where she'd last seen the demon.

"We got him," Phoebe affirmed.

"That was a lot easier than I thought it was going to be," Paige said, pushing her hair out of her face.

"Easy?" Piper asked unbelievingly, looking at the chaos around her. She stood painfully and crossed to a vase that had fallen on the ground and broken into several pieces. "We're going to need glue," she noted glumly.

"You're going to need a lot of glue," Paige said with a derisive snort. "Best to just let it go."

1

Phoebe cleared her throat meaningfully and dropped her eyes.

"What?" Paige asked. "What mystical history does it have that I'm not aware of?"

"It's not that, sweetie. It's just that Dad gave this to Mom on their last anniversary," Phoebe said quietly.

"It came with a dozen red roses. They seemed to bloom forever," Piper added.

"Well, that's what we thought—until Prue caught Dad replacing them every few days," Phoebe said, laughing with Piper at the warm memory.

At the mention of Prue, Phoebe and Piper's oldest sister, Paige grew quiet. Phoebe, Piper, and Prue had all discovered they were witches at the same time. They were the Charmed Ones, and they had a great destiny. Paige herself was a late arrival to the game. She was Phoebe and Piper's half sister, the daughter of their mother and her Whitelighter. It was only recently, after Prue had been killed by a demon, that Paige had discovered her sisters and embarked upon the life of a Charmed One.

Paige cleared her throat. "Well, I hate to break up all this reminiscing, but I have to get to work."

"Ah yes, the busy life of a social worker, saving kids, helping families," Phoebe said, forcing a smile.

"Okay, so it's not glamorous work, but at least I get to help people," Paige said.

Piper barely heard them. She stared at the broken pieces of the vase and promised herself she wouldn't get upset, or at least not more upset than she was already. She sighed and closed her eyes, shutting out the memories of her parents' broken marriage as she shut out the image of the broken vase. "Just once I'd like to have a peaceful day. No work, no errands, no demons to fight."

"Yes, but only *one* day. You wouldn't want life to get boring," Phoebe teased as she shoved the sofa back into place.

"Right now, boring doesn't sound so bad," Piper answered. She opened her eyes and began to try to piece together the bone china vase. Behind her, Phoebe was picking up chairs and straightening things up. Paige left through the front door with a quick farewell.

Some days it wasn't easy being a witch. *I could do for a while without magic powers and a great destiny,* Piper thought.

"There's a piece missing," she said at last, staring at the shattered mess of shards in front of her.

Suddenly Leo, Piper's husband and the sisters' Whitelighter, orbed into the room in a cloud of shimmering light.

"What did I miss?" he asked.

"Everything," Piper said.

"Did you vanquish the demon?" he asked.

"Yes, but not before he vanquished Mom's vase."

"Huh?"

"Mom's vase. There's a piece missing. Help me look for it," Piper said, crawling carefully along the floor.

"That wouldn't be it over there, would it?" Leo asked, wincing.

Piper looked up to follow his gaze and saw the missing bit of the vase. It was lodged firmly into a painting on the wall, dead center between the eyes of the young lady depicted in it.

"Ah, crap," Piper said.

Grocery shopping was Piper's latest solution to stress, whether supernatural or human. As an ex-chef, food was important to her, not only as a source of nutrition, but also as a source of comfort.

"What kind of cookies do you want to bake?" Leo asked, pushing the cart beside her.

"Chocolate fudge chip," Piper said, glancing at him sideways. She was fully aware of how ridiculous it was for a Whitelighter to be out grocery shopping with no higher purpose. *But surely our marriage is a higher purpose,* she thought. *Heaven knows we need the time together and a little shred of normalcy in our lives.*

"So, do you want to continue our conversation from earlier?" Leo asked.

Piper had to bite her lip to keep from telling him just how much she didn't want to finish that particular conversation. In fact, unless it had the words *chocolate* or *cookies* in it, she didn't want to have *any* conversation. Instead she took a deep breath. "I just don't know if I'm prepared for children, Leo."

"I'm not sure that anyone is truly *prepared*, Piper. You just have to be ready to open up your heart."

"And take on responsibility for yet another life."

"It would be *our* responsibility," he reminded her.

She laughed. "I can just imagine you changing diapers and burping a baby."

"For starters. Then there's the part where they grow up. You get to mold a young mind, teach them right from wrong, and eventually watch them with pride as they start a family of their own."

"Have you been talking to Dad?" Piper asked suspiciously.

"No."

"Then maybe you should, just to know what you're getting into."

"I think I know what I'm getting into. Besides, your father's still not that comfortable with me."

"That's going to have to change if we're thinking about having children," she said.

"He and I can work things out," Leo reassured her, looking determined.

Piper hid a grin behind her hand. *That'll be the*

day! she thought. She wiped the thought from her mind and returned to the discussion. "I don't know, our lives are just so chaotic. Demons, warlocks, Phoebe's boyfriends. Are you serious about bringing a child into a world, into a *home*, that sees all of that?"

"As long as you're in that world, and that *home*, then I am serious."

Why does he have to always turn things on me like that so he seems like the sweet, romantic one, and I seem like the selfish, uncaring shrew? Piper sighed and said, "I just don't think I'm ready to be a—"

"Mama!"

Piper jumped as something collided with her leg. She glanced down, her hands moving into a defensive posture, ready to freeze her attacker in a nanosecond.

A small child stared up at her, spittle dribbling down its chin. The front of its romper was wet, and its tiny hands, gleaming with a sticky-looking red substance, kneaded the leg of Piper's black rayon pants.

She shook her head slightly, nose crinkling in disgust. "Leo," she whispered. "Get it off me."

"Ah, hi there, little fellow," Leo cooed, already kneeling beside it.

"Don't talk to it, get rid of it!" she shrieked.

"Piper, it's a child, not a demon," Leo said condescendingly. "You don't just get rid of it."

The little boy swayed back and forth as he

stared at Leo. A smile turned up the corners of his mouth and he began to giggle and drool even more incessantly.

"You're a good boy, aren't you?" Leo said, reaching out to tickle his tummy. "Where's your mommy?"

"Just because he likes you doesn't mean we can keep him," Piper said sarcastically.

"There you are!" a woman cried, running up to them with a look of relief on her face. "Samuel, don't wander off from Mommy again."

She scooped the boy up in her arms. "Sorry," she said, barely even glancing at Piper. She carried her son back to her abandoned shopping cart and put the child inside.

"All children like me," Leo said as he straightened up.

"Let me guess," Piper said. "It's because you're a Whitelighter, right?"

"Pretty much. But I've always had a way with children and animals."

"Of course you have," Piper responded. In her mind she envisioned endless years stretching before her, being hated by her children as the "bad parent" while Leo was loved and adored not only by their children, but also by their children's friends and pets. "I hate being the villain," she muttered.

"What was that?"

Piper took a deep breath. "You *really* want one of those?" she asked, gesturing toward the drooling toddler, who was still sitting in his mother's grocery cart waving at Leo.

"Yes. Don't you?" Leo asked, eyes burning into her.

Piper sighed and cocked her head to the side. "I don't know. I mean, maybe someday, sure. But now just doesn't feel like the right time."

"When will be the right time?" Leo asked. Piper walked next to him as he pushed the shopping cart down the paper goods aisle.

"Oh, I don't know, like in twenty years when we've killed all the demons in the world and our lives have become seminormal."

Leo stopped. Grabbing Piper's arm, he pulled her around to face him. "You know that's never going to happen, right?"

Piper refused to look him in the eyes. "I know," she said, her throat tight. "No matter how hard we work, there will always be more demons."

"That's not what I meant and you know it," Leo said, lowering his voice and glancing quickly around. "Our lives are never going to be normal."

Tears stung the back of Piper's eyes. "I guess. But I'm not asking for things to be perfectly normal, just seminormal."

"I know," Leo said, pulling her to him and folding her in his arms. "That's why we're here in the grocery store."

"At least we can shop together like a normal

couple," Piper said, relaxing slightly and enjoying the feel of his soft cotton shirt beneath her cheek. Luckily there was no one else in their aisle—normal couples shopped in grocery stores, sure, but hugged in them? Not so much.

A sudden wailing filled the air and Piper jerked away from her husband, throwing her hands over her ears and looking frantically around.

"Or maybe not," Leo shouted over the din.

"What's going on?" Piper asked.

"It's the children, they're crying."

"All over the store?"

"It sounds like all over the city," Leo answered. "I've got to go."

Before she could open her mouth to protest he was gone.

"Great," Piper said. She glanced around her. "Just great."

No one seemed to have noticed Leo's exit, so Piper decided to make one of her own. She abandoned her cart in the middle of an aisle and dashed outside.

As she left, hands still pressed over her ears, she nearly bumped into an old man who was trying to enter the store. "Sorry," she muttered.

"Not at all," the old man said, smiling kindly.

Leo was right. All the children were crying. There were children crying in the parking lot and she could see one crying across the street. *What is going on?* Piper thought. She got into her car and slammed the door. It only slightly muffled the sound, so she flicked the radio on and turned it up loud.

"Piper! Did you pick up that hand lotion for me?" Phoebe asked, bounding down the stairs.

Piper closed the door and then leaned back against it, shoulders slumped in defeat. It had been a bad morning and she wasn't prepared to deal with anything else just yet.

"Sweetie? What's wrong?" Phoebe asked, sounding concerned.

Piper looked like she was going to cry. "Oh, nothing, just a store full of screaming kids. Maybe even a whole city full of them. Leo pulled a vanishing act while we were shopping and I couldn't stand the noise, so I have to try shopping again sometime later. Much later."

Phoebe crinkled her nose up and looked at her frustrated sister. "So much for a quiet day doing boring married-people stuff," she teased, trying to keep her tone light.

"Yeah."

"Well, that's okay. I have to go to work for a little while. I can swing by the store on my way home. What do you need me to pick up?"

"Nothing."

"Come on, this is me, offering to help, offering to shop for boring things. As your sister I have to advise you to take me up on my offer." Phoebe tossed Piper her best perky smile, but her older sister just dragged herself away from the door.

"Forget it," Piper said, moving into the living room and abandoning her purse on the floor. She sunk down on the couch and leaned her head back.

"Hey, it's going to be okay," Phoebe said, following quickly to sit beside her sister.

"How do you know?" Piper asked.

"Because I had a vision," Phoebe said teasingly.

Piper hit her with a pillow. "Stop."

"Well, I could have, you never know," Phoebe said.

"Oh, if it only worked that way. There are days I would do anything to use our powers for personal gain," Piper moaned, closing her eyes again.

Phoebe knew exactly what Piper meant. She herself had felt that way many times. She had also learned first-hand the dangers of acting on those desires. She leaned over and hugged her sister.

"Okay, so I didn't have a vision. But I do have something even stronger than that."

"What?" Piper asked.

"Faith, silly."

Piper laughed.

"Seriously, Piper," Phoebe said. "I have faith that everything is going to work out for you and Leo. It has to. The two of you have survived too much to let anything stand in your way. Even your desire to live a normal life."

"I guess you're right. I hope so."

"I am," Phoebe said. She kissed Piper on the forehead and bounded to her feet. "Now I have to get to work. Sure you don't want me to stop by the store?"

"I'm sure," Piper said with a wave of her hand.

Phoebe walked down the front steps and jumped into her car, thinking about Piper. Her sister's sadness really bothered Phoebe, especially since she was an advice columnist. Letters poured in from all over the Bay Area from people who wanted to "Ask Phoebe" something, and she would reply with a witty, insightful, simple answer. She sighed, thinking about it. *If only I had simple answers for us. Our lives are just too complicated. Besides, not one of my readers has ever written in asking if they should continue to date a man once they discovered that he was a demon or an angel. I swear, there are days when I don't even believe our lives.*

"Are you sure about this?" Paige asked, leaning back in her chair at work as she played with the telephone cord.

"Positive. I can't use the ticket," Tina said.

"Well, thanks. I haven't been to the symphony since I was a little girl."

"Then go, and enjoy yourself."

"I think I will."

"I'll leave the ticket for you at the box office."

"Great, thanks. I owe you one," Paige said.

"No prob, Paige," Tina responded. "I gotta go. Have fun!"

Paige hung up the phone and settled back into her chair. *The symphony.* Her adoptive parents had taken her several times when she was little until she had thrown a temper tantrum and told them she hated it. For years after their death she had wanted to go back but had never found the time. When Tina had mentioned she had symphony tickets she couldn't use, Paige was thrilled. She was so thrilled, in fact, that she cancelled her dinner plans for the following night. It had been long enough since she'd been to the symphony.

She looked at the clock and stood up. *Wait until Piper and Phoebe hear what I get to do tomorrow night,* she thought.

On her afternoon break Paige found herself humming. The day had started in horror but was ending in beauty. *Just the way I like it,* she thought. She was definitely not a morning person.

Piper was giving the grocery store another try, this time without Leo. She had managed to make it all the way to the checkout stand without incident. Still, she kept glancing over her shoulder, feeling like something was there, watching her.

You're being paranoid, she told herself, beginning to unload the contents of her cart. Suddenly the hair on the back of her neck rose on end. She turned around slowly and came face-to-face with a pair of wide blue eyes. Six inches away was a baby, staring at her. She took a hasty step back and the infant leaned forward in her mother's arms, reaching for Piper.

"She likes you," the baby's mother said.

"No, no," Piper protested. "Babies always hate me. Love my husband, hate me."

"Well, this one certainly thinks differently. Do you want to hold her?"

"No, thank you," Piper said hastily. *What kind of a mother would offer her child to a total stranger?* she thought. She turned away and greeted the checker. Behind her, the baby started to cry and Piper winced.

Outside she unlocked the car and put the groceries in. She returned the cart quickly and ducked into her car just as the woman with the infant was coming out.

She gunned the engine and took off, escaping any further interaction with babies—or with anyone who had one.

After she parked the car in front of the Manor and got out, she opened the door to the backseat and stepped back, stunned at what she saw. There, with his hand inside one of her bags of groceries, was a young red-haired boy.

Bewildered, Piper glanced from side to side before turning back to the child. "Okay, who are you and where did you come from?"

"Jimmy."

"Jimmy? Your name is Jimmy? Okay, Jimmy, where is your mommy?"

"I don't know."

"How did you get here?"

"I don't know."

"Where do you live?"

"I don't know."

"Then what do you know?" Piper asked, frustrated.

Jimmy stared up at her silently.

Piper pressed her hands to her head. *I don't need this right now,* she thought to herself. She looked at Jimmy. "All right, let's go inside while I figure this out."

She held the door open wide and he clambered out. She picked up her bags and headed to the front door with Jimmy behind her. Halfway up the steps she stopped. Sitting on her welcome mat was Samuel, the child Leo had played with that morning in the grocery store.

"What on earth?" Piper muttered.

She opened the door and stumbled inside. The kids fell in behind her. She threw the groceries in the direction of the kitchen before crouching down on the floor and grabbing both children by the arms.

"Where are your mommies?" she asked.

They both just shook their heads and stared at her with wide eyes.

She rocked back on her heels. "This isn't

happening. Paige, Phoebe, are you home?" she called. Only silence greeted her.

"Leo! Get your bu—" She paused, glancing at the children. "Get your tushy down here right now, mister."

"Tushy? Piper, are you feeling okay?" Leo asked as he orbed in.

"Do I look like I'm feeling okay?" she asked, scrambling to her feet.

"Actually—" Noticing the kids, Leo stopped in midsentence. "Where did they come from?"

"That is what I was about to ask you," Piper said, narrowing her eyes. "I found one of them in my car and the other on our porch. They don't know how they got here, where home is, or who their mommies are."

"That one looks like Samuel, the boy from the grocery store."

"That's because he is."

"I don't understand."

"Neither do I. And that's not all. There was a baby girl in the store staring at me."

"Maybe she was just drawn to your beautiful smile," Leo said lightly.

"What smile?" Piper asked with a frown.

"Right," he answered hastily. "Well, I'll go, uh . . . call the Elders. From the kitchen."

"Wait! What am I supposed to do with these kids?"

Leo smiled. "Return them to their parents."

Piper choked back a scream as he headed

toward the kitchen, but orbed out as soon as he was sure the little boys couldn't see. "Leo, if you had something to do with this, I swear you'll be sorry," she shouted, shaking her fist at the air. Turning to the kids, she ordered, "Okay, everyone, back to the grocery store. Hopefully your mommies will be there looking for you."

She grabbed Jimmy and Samuel by the hands and headed back outside to the car.

"I need car seat," Samuel sputtered as she tried to put him in the backseat.

"Aunty Piper doesn't have one of those," she said with a sigh.

"He can't go without it," Jimmy informed her.

"And what about you? You seem to have made it here just fine without one," Piper said, hands on her hips.

"He's littler," Jimmy said solemnly.

"Great. Where am I going to find a car seat?"

Jimmy just shrugged. A thought occurred to her and she glanced around. They were alone on the street. She opened the front passenger door. "Here, you two sit in here for just a minute while Aunty Piper finds a car seat."

The children clambered inside and Piper shut the door behind them. She stepped back and took a deep breath. *Okay, you can do this, no big deal.*

"My need is great, the children small, I need a seat for this kid . . . kid . . . kid not so . . . tall." She waited.

Nothing.

"Oh, come on, can't I get a break?" Piper moaned.

Just then a station wagon drove slowly by and stopped four houses down. Piper tilted her head to the side. "Not what I had in mind, but it could work."

Waving at the kids to stay where they were, Piper hurried up the street. A young woman with curly blonde hair—one of the neighbors—was just stepping out of the car when Piper reached her.

"Hi," Piper said, searching her memory in vain for the woman's name.

"Hi, Piper, isn't it?"

"Yes," Piper said, relieved that the woman recognized her.

"I'm Bonnie," the woman prompted.

Piper smiled her best innocent smile. "I know, Bonnie."

"What's going on?" Bonnie asked as she opened the back door and began to undo the safety restraints on a car seat holding a gurgling toddler.

"Actually, I have a huge favor to ask," Piper confessed. "I'm watching my cousin's children for her. Turns out she needs me to drop them off at their grandmother's house, but she forgot to leave a car seat for me."

"Say no more," Bonnie said. "How long do you need to borrow it for?"

"Just an hour, two max," Piper said. "Thank you, I really appreciate this."

"Well, I'm all about child safety," Bonnie told her with a perky smile. "I'm sure you'd do the same for me."

"Of course," Piper answered, putting on her best saccharine smile.

"Have you ever installed a child seat before?"

"No, but how hard could it be?"

Bonnie didn't answer; she just started laughing. The sound unnerved Piper, who was already on edge. Giggling hysterically, Bonnie pulled her child out of the car seat and handed her to Piper.

"Here, hold Jessica. You're going to need help," Bonnie said.

Piper started to protest, but Bonnie held up her hand. "No, you really don't want to try this on your own without a manual, diagram, or extra pair of hands."

"Taking care of kids, or installing a car seat?" Piper asked wryly as she stared at Jessica.

"Both," Bonnie said. She leaned over inside the car and made a few grunting noises before straightening up and pulling out the child seat. "Let's go put this in your car," she said.

Piper led the way, suddenly feeling vulnerable. She hoped the kids didn't take the opportunity to blow her cover and alert Bonnie to the fact that something weird was going on.

Piper watched as Bonnie's hands flew, buckling the seat belt into places on the child seat

Piper would never even have thought of. At last Bonnie picked up Samuel and buckled him in. Miraculously, he said nothing.

"What about you?" Bonnie asked Jimmy.

"I'm sixty-one pounds. I'm a big boy."

"Yes, you are. It's a good thing, too. I don't think I have a car seat that would fit you."

"Bonnie, thanks for your help. I think I can manage from here," Piper said, holding Jessica out in front of her.

"No problem," Bonnie said, taking her daughter.

The grocery store was a short trip from Halliwell Manor, but it felt like it took forever. Along the way, Piper fell victim to an increasing sense of paranoia. Every few seconds she checked her rearview mirror to make sure the children were okay and not multiplying. Aside from a lot of fidgeting, they seemed fine.

When she pulled into the parking lot she saw a police car. A woman was talking with a police officer, using wild gestures. *I bet that's Jimmy's mom*, Piper thought. She slowed down and pulled into a parking stall close by.

"Excuse me, but did you lose a child?" Piper asked, rolling down her window.

"Yes, yes, I did. Someone took my Jimmy!" the lady wailed.

"Ah, good. You see, when I got home, I found a stowaway in my backseat," Piper said. "He answers to the name of Jimmy."

She got out of the car, opened the back door

and Jimmy jumped out. "Hi, Mom!" he shouted.

"Jimmy!" the woman shrieked, flying forward and scooping her son up in her arms.

"You say he stowed away in your backseat?" the police officer asked, walking over to Piper.

"Yes. I got home, opened the back door to get the groceries and there he was. I came right back, hoping to find someone who knew him."

"Jimmy, why did you get in that lady's car?"

"Don't know," the little boy said with a shrug. "I liked her. I climbed in and she didn't see me."

"Never, ever do that again. You had Mommy worried to death! What if something had happened to you?" Jimmy's mother asked, sobbing.

"I'm sorry, Mommy."

"Thank you, ma'am. I wish all missing child reports ended this happily," the police officer told Piper.

"No problem. I'm just glad Jimmy's back where he belongs. If you'll excuse me now, I really must get home."

Sobbing hysterically, Jimmy's mother thanked her again and Piper quickly excused herself and hopped in her car, eager to get out of there. One stray child in her car could be explained, but the second would be a challenge.

She pulled out of the parking lot. *Now, what should I do with the other one?* she wondered. She checked her rearview mirror and the sight of the police car gave her an idea.

She made it to a police station quickly, but it took Piper a while to get Samuel out of the car seat. At last he came free, and she carried him into the station.

She walked up to the desk and addressed the officer behind it. "Excuse me, I need some help."

"Yes, ma'am?"

"I found this little guy wandering around by himself. I looked to see if I could find his parents, but he seemed to be alone. He said his name is Samuel."

"You've come to the right place," the officer behind the counter assured her. He reached out and took Samuel from her arms. "We had a report just a few minutes ago that a little boy matching his description wandered off from his mother."

"Great, thank you," Piper said, edging toward the door.

"Who can I tell them found him?" the officer asked.

"I'd really rather remain anonymous," Piper said.

"There might be a reward," the officer prompted, looking quizzically at her.

Piper forced herself to smile. "You keep it. I'm just an average citizen doing what anyone would have done. Bye." She waved to Samuel and left.

Outside, she breathed a sigh of relief. *I'm glad that's over!* she thought.

When she reached her neighborhood she parked by Bonnie's house so her neighbor could help her take the car seat out.

"I really appreciate it," Piper said as Bonnie undid all the straps.

"Any time," Bonnie answered with a cheerful smile. "That's what neighbors are for."

"Yes," Piper said, "that's what I've heard." She gritted her teeth. A normal person with a normal life and nothing to hide would have offered to return the favor at some point. Piper couldn't. "Well, thanks again," she said, feeling awkward.

"No problem," Bonnie said, waving as she headed off to her own car with the car seat.

"What's for dinner?" Phoebe asked as Piper walked into the house.

"Liver—yours, if you ask me that again," Piper muttered, dragging herself toward the kitchen.

"Cranky. What happened to you after I left?" Phoebe asked, following behind her sister.

"Plenty."

Phoebe hopped up onto the counter, putting on her best listening face. Piper dropped into a chair with a weary sigh.

The front door opened again, and after a moment Paige bounced into the kitchen, looking far too perky for Piper's taste.

"What's for dinner?" Paige asked.

Piper's eyes narrowed dangerously. "Liver."

"Fortunate for me, unfortunate for you," Phoebe said with a smirk.

"What is that supposed to mean?" Paige asked, getting herself a glass of water.

"Piper is *not* having a good day."

"Ah, then it's pizza," Paige said. "Pepperoni?"

"Vegetarian," Phoebe countered.

Paige leaned against the counter, sipping her water. Piper was too tired to care what kind of pizza they ordered, let alone participate in the debate about it.

"Ooh, or we could get Chinese food," Paige said. "The new delivery guy is awfully cute."

"You're in a good mood," Phoebe noted.

"That's because I'm going to the symphony tomorrow night," Paige announced.

The symphony. That sounds nice. I can't remember the last time Leo and I did something romantic like that, Piper thought.

"Ooh, what are you going to wear?" Phoebe asked.

"I don't know, I hadn't really thought about it," Paige said.

"Ha, then you'd better start," Piper said.

"Really?" Paige asked.

"Yes, really," Phoebe answered. "You can't wear just anything. It would be uncivilized."

"Quite," Piper agreed, flashing a haughty smile.

"Okay. Maybe one of you can help me go through my closet tonight," Paige said.

"So, what happened to you today?" Phoebe asked, turning to Piper.

"Children."

"Children?" Paige asked.

"Lots and lots of children."

Chapter

2

The next day Piper spent all morning at P3, the club she owned, going over the books and placing orders. Things seemed to be going well, which was good news. She had managed to get in touch with the manager for the band that would be playing at the club for the entire weekend. Better still, the manager knew who she was and even had his charges prepared.

Thank goodness, I was in no mood to deal with a double booking, or an outbreak of laryngitis, she thought. *All in all, this is turning out to be a much better day*.

At a little after one she decided to head home for a couple of hours, planning to return to the club in the evening to touch base with her bartender. *Then I think I might just take the rest of the night off, soak in the bathtub, read a good book, maybe get in some cuddle time if I can clip someone's wings for an hour.*

As she got in the car the radio station started playing one of her favorite songs. She smiled and settled back in the seat. Even the traffic was mercifully light and the drive was a quick one. Once home, Piper climbed the stairs to the front of the house still singing, though much more softly than she had been when inside the car. There were no neighbors about, but she still felt shy about singing in public. Just as she reached the door to the house, though, she heard a sound behind her—a very tiny sound.

Realizing with a touch of panic, more about the singing than anything else, that she was not alone, Piper twisted around. What she saw caused her heart to sink. "Oh no," she gasped.

There, crouched behind her at the bottom of the steps, was another little kid. He had a dirt-streaked face and the biggest eyes she had ever seen.

"Go home," she hissed, waving her hand at him.

He didn't move.

"Shoo, scat, go," she said, gesturing more emphatically.

He edged closer to her.

"No, you're not coming in. Where are your mommy and daddy?"

The boy scooted closer still but said nothing.

"What is your name?"

Now he was clinging to her leg. She tried to gently shake him off, but he only held on harder. She finally reached down and pried his hands off of her. She hurried down the steps to the street and looked around frantically.

There was no sign of anyone. "Anyone missing a child?" she called.

With a sigh of defeat she finally turned back around. She opened the door and he scampered in before her.

"Whoa, what do we have here?" Phoebe asked, coming down the stairs.

"One of my shadows," Piper said, grimacing.

"You sing pretty," the little boy sputtered.

"You sang for him?" Phoebe asked, amusement written all over her face.

"Not now, Phoebe," Piper said, glaring at her.

"You won't even sing for me, and I'm family," Phoebe teased.

"Phoebe, a little help here, please?" Piper hissed.

"I don't know, Piper," Phoebe said, smiling. "You've got a little fan there. I don't want to break this up."

"Phoebe!"

Suddenly the boy screamed at the top of his lungs, and both girls jumped.

Downtown in a fancy boutique, Paige had problems. *Dress* problems, to be exact. She stood in front of the store's full-length mirror holding four different dresses. A saleswoman wearing an expensively tailored suit and a look of frustration was valiantly trying to help her. She and Paige were the only ones in the shop.

"Okay, we've narrowed it down," Paige said, more to herself than to Mary, the hapless employee. "We've got the white strappy one," she said, holding the dress up to herself. Short and tight, it was a curve hugger, with dozens of tiny straps criss-crossed across her shoulders and back.

"We've got the sultry red one," she said, picking up a red dress that was floor-length but slit almost up to her hip.

"We've got the provocative green one," she said, holding up a backless, strapless green dress that was long and elegant.

"Or there's the classic black." She held the black dress against her. It boasted a scoop neckline, short skirt, and long, sheer sleeves.

"It's been an hour, they all look great on you, just pick one," Mary finally wailed, pushed past her limit by Paige's indecision.

"But I don't want to pick the wrong one. I want to look great for the symphony."

"You're going to the symphony *tonight*, right?"

"Yes."

"So, you need to make a decision in the next five minutes in order to have enough time to change, do your hair and makeup, and get there."

Paige glanced at the clock on the wall. "Yeah, you're right."

"Then here," Mary said, struggling to her feet. She grabbed the white dress from Paige and threw it on a chair. "Too much work to put on."

She pulled the red one away and said, "Too slutty."

Then she snatched the green one from Paige's hands before she could even protest the first two decisions. "You'll freeze to death in this."

Mary slapped the black dress with the back of her hand. "Go with black. Classic, elegant. You'll look great and you won't stick out like a sore thumb."

"Thanks," Paige said, nodding as she slowly realized the wisdom of what Mary was saying. "I'll take it."

"That's it? You listened to me? I should have told you what to buy an hour ago."

"Yeah, you should have," Paige said, patting her condescendingly on the arm. She could see Mary's annoyance growing, but nothing was going to ruin Paige's evening. Besides, Mary's job was to deal with fussy customers, and Paige couldn't possibly be the worst. *After all*, she thought, *I know Phoebe shops here.*

A half hour later Piper and Phoebe were no closer to getting an answer about the child's identity. With the exception of telling Piper she sang pretty, he hadn't said a word. Piper wasn't sure if he couldn't talk, or just wouldn't. She had given him some milk and filled Phoebe in on the events of her day. Phoebe had only smirked during the telling, which did not improve Piper's mood.

"So, what are you going to name him?" Phoebe asked.

"Name him? Nooo. We're not keeping him," Piper protested, crossing her arms over her chest.

"Well, we'd better figure out something soon," Phoebe said, eyebrows arching. "Because he's jumped on all the furniture and now he's in the corner making a mess."

"What do you mean, in the corner making a mess?" Piper asked.

Phoebe gestured and Piper followed her pointing finger. There, in the corner, the little boy was quietly throwing up.

"No! Stop . . . uh . . . whatever your name is!" Piper shouted, running to him. "We don't do this here. We go to the bathroom."

"Best to just let him finish, Piper. Otherwise you'll be cleaning up the hall as well."

As much as Piper hated to admit it, she knew Phoebe was right. Biting back a scream of frustration, Piper set the child back down, careful not to get any little-boy vomit on her clothes.

She straightened up slowly, fighting back the urge to get sick from the smell. "That's it, I don't want kids. Ever."

"Well, that's kind of harsh. What would Leo say to that?" Phoebe asked.

"He would object. Leo *wants* to have kids."

"Really? I'd love to be Aunt Phoebe."

"The problem is, I don't think I'll love being Mommy." Piper glanced down at the little boy. He finally seemed to be finished throwing up. He scampered off and she stood for a moment, staring at the mess.

"You'll be a great mother," Phoebe said.

"You really think so?"

"I do," Phoebe answered, her voice serious. "And I think you'll know when you're ready."

"It won't be anytime soon, I can tell you that," Piper said, walking to the kitchen to get some wet paper towels.

As Piper walked back into the living room, Phoebe said, "You might be surprised. I hear the little suckers can grow on you." She was making faces at the little boy, who was laughing excitedly.

"Great, Phoebe, make him feel at home. Now we'll never get him to leave."

"He'll leave when he's ready. I'm guessing in about fourteen years or so, when he goes to college."

"Very funny. Just for that," Piper said handing Phoebe the paper towels, "you can clean up after him."

"Gee, Mom, I'd love to, but I really have to get going."

"Phoebe Halliwell, don't you dare leave me

here alone with him," Piper shouted as Phoebe dashed for the door.

"Whoops! I think these are yours," Phoebe said from outside, just before the door closed.

"What? Phoebe, get back here!" Piper followed her sister, but Phoebe was too quick. She was driving away by the time Piper got to the door.

But that was the least of Piper's problems. Three little girls stood on the stoop, staring up at her. One of them carried a small child's keyboard, another a tiny guitar, and the third had a tamborine. "'Hail, hail, the gang's all here,'" Piper noted through gritted teeth. "I don't suppose any of you has a name?"

Paige paid for the dress and made her way home. At the Manor, she found a mess.

"Piper? What's going on?" Paige asked as she surveyed the papers scattered all over the floor. Above her, she could hear the sound of many running feet.

"Paige, thank heavens you're here. You have to help me," Piper said, running in from the other room. Her features were strained and she kept pushing a lock of hair out of her eye, but it refused to stay put. Piper glared at the strand of hair. "Scissors," she hissed. "That'll fix my problem." She turned and headed straight for the kitchen.

"Ah, Piper," Paige said, stepping forward quickly and grabbing her sister by her shoulders.

"Cutting your own hair? Never a good idea. Especially when you're upset. And when did you decide to open a day care center?"

"Paige, you have to help me, I'm going crazy. There are children everywhere—" Piper broke off in midsentence, her eyes going wide in terror.

"No!" she screamed. "Put that down!"

She raced off and Paige turned just in time to see her sister yanking a jar of who-knew-what out of the hands of a young girl. Paige couldn't tell what was in the jar, but knew by the look of the jar itself that it wasn't a harmless spice the kids had found in the kitchen.

Paige lifted her eyebrows and silently mouthed "Okay" to herself before beating a hasty retreat upstairs to the bathroom. Once there, she locked herself in and quickly showered. She found herself humming as she did her makeup and put her hair up on top of her head.

A heavy pounding on the door made her jump suddenly enough to jab her scalp hard with a bobby pin.

"Bathroom!" a small, boyish voice screamed.

Paige turned back to the mirror, but the pounding only became louder, more frantic. At last she gave up.

"All right, already," she said, flinging the door open.

Paige cringed as a small boy raced past on his way to the toilet. His pants were already around his ankles.

"Yikes," Paige said, hastily vacating the bathroom, closing the door behind her to give the kid some privacy. "Now there's something you don't see every day," she said.

She dashed into her room, changed, and grabbed a pair of black slingback heels. She did one quick twirl in front of her mirror and smiled in satisfaction.

"Paige!" Piper yelled.

Paige winced and opened her bedroom door a crack. Piper was walking down the hall away from her. *Perfect.* She left her room, carrying her shoes, and crept quietly toward the front door. She knew she should stay and help her sister, but she just couldn't. She'd spent too much money on her dress to wear it while cleaning up after a bunch of kids.

Her hand was on the knob when she heard a voice behind her ask, "Where are you going?"

"Shh," Paige said, spinning around to face her accuser, a young girl in a pink dress.

The little girl only narrowed her eyes. "I'm going to tell on you!"

"No, wait!" Paige whispered.

It was no use. The little girl turned and ran for the other room, ponytail bobbing behind her. The jig was up. Abandoning stealth, Paige flung open the door and ran outside.

The doorbell rang, and Piper, who was standing in the kitchen, trying to catch her breath, jumped.

"What now?" she said. Leaning back against the refrigerator, she gazed at the sea of grubby faces around her. "Everyone, stay. Here. No one move, okay?"

Only uncomprehending stares answered her. "Oh, forget it," she said, throwing up her hands in frustration.

Making her way over several crawling bodies, she finally reached the door—after tripping twice— and flung it open. "Go home!" she shouted.

"Uh, Piper, you okay?"

"Darryl! I'm so sorry," Piper said, staring at the tall police officer in mild surprise. "I wasn't expecting you."

"Yeah, I got that. Can I come in?"

"Sure. What's going on?" she asked, opening the door wider and stepping back.

"I tried calling, but your phone's off the hook. It seems there've been a rash of kidnappings all over the city. Dozens of children have turned up missing. It's like an epidemic."

"Interesting. Any idea what's causing it?"

"No. But for some reason I thought you might," he said, stepping inside. "This seems more super than natural."

Piper closed the door and led him into the living room. "Well, you came to the right place, but I'm afraid I don't have any answers for you. Just more questions."

Darryl stopped in his tracks, his mouth gaping

as he took in the crowd of children. "Where . . . how . . . are these the missing kids?"

"All excellent questions, Darryl, and I'm so glad you're here to help answer them."

"Wait, I know him," Darryl exclaimed, pointing to a little blond boy pounding on the floor with chopsticks. He reached into his pocket and fished out a picture of the child.

Piper took the picture and stared at it for a moment. The resemblance was unmistakable. She flipped the picture over. *Donny, age four.* "Donny, age four, you stop that this instant!" she called.

The little boy looked up, eyes wide, and dropped the chopsticks. "Music pretty," he pouted before shoving his thumb into his mouth.

"It looks like these are your missing kids, Darryl. Which means *you* get to take them all home."

"What? Why me?" he asked.

"You're the detective. You can at least make up something reasonable to tell their parents."

"And you can't?"

Piper let out a short, sarcastic laugh. "No, because somehow 'Gee, your kid seemed to follow me home' doesn't sound right even to me. So, you take care of them, and I'm going to consult the Book of Shadows."

She was halfway to the stairs before Darryl asked, "What about your sisters?"

"Well, they both had better things to do. Convenient for them."

"*I've* got better things to do," Darryl protested.

"No you don't," she called back over her shoulder.

Once in the attic Piper shut the door behind her with a grateful *thud*. "At least I can't hear their little voices up here," she told herself as she crossed to the Book.

The attic was crammed with old furniture, clothes, boxes, and the memories of several lifetimes. It was always a place of comfort and sanctuary. It was also a place of answers, answers that Piper desperately needed. The Book of Shadows contained spells and information on every demon, warlock, and magical creature that had been encountered by the Charmed Ones' witch ancestors for centuries. *The book must have something*, she thought.

She opened it and began flipping through the pages. Within moments she heard little fists knocking on the door. "Pwiper, let us in," a tiny voice warbled.

"Not now, go see Uncle Darryl," she called forcefully.

There was silence, and then sniffling outside. She waited a minute, hoping it would subside, but the crying only seemed to get louder. "Oh, for heaven's sake," she said, striding to the door. She flung it open and froze the six tearful children who stood on the other side.

She heard heavy steps pounding on the stairs. "Kids, come back! Leave Aunty Piper alone."

"Aunty?" Piper asked, eyebrow arched, as Darryl dove into view.

"Could be worse," he gasped. "It could be 'Mommy.' How'd you like to have this many kids?"

"Not so much," she answered.

Darryl stared at the frozen children. "Was that really necessary?"

"Yes," Piper stated matter-of-factly. "Now, shoo. I've got work to do, and there are a dozen more kids downstairs who need looking after."

"Make that fourteen."

"Excuse me?"

"Two more just showed up at your door."

"Darryl, you let them in?"

"What was I supposed to do, leave them standing out there?"

"Yes! Again!" Piper told him, unable to keep the desperation she was feeling from her voice.

"Twins, three years old at most. Right. Besides, it looks like you've done a great job of keeping them out yourself," Darryl said, an edge of sarcasm in his words.

Piper stomped her foot and thought about freezing Darryl as well. Just then, though, she heard a crash from downstairs. She growled deep in her throat. "Go take care of that, or they're all going to take a very long time to defrost."

Darryl shook his head at her before heading
back downstairs. Piper closed the door again,
leaving the frozen children outside.

After a few minutes of flipping pages, she
sighed and closed the book. "I don't even know
what it is I'm looking for." *What could be causing
the children to follow me? Is it a spell?* The house
shook slightly. *Maybe some horrific new form of
demonic torture?*

"Leo!" she called.

"Still working on it, hon," her husband
announced as he orbed in.

Another crash from downstairs and the dis-
tinct sound of Darryl shouting drifted up to them.

"Any chance you can work faster?" Piper
hissed.

Leo just shook his head. "Anything in the
Book of Shadows?"

"I don't know. I can't even figure out what to
look for."

"Maybe Phoebe and Paige can help."

"Phoebe and Paige. Sure, what a great idea.
Why didn't I think of that?" she said sarcastically. "Oh, wait . . . I did. Huh. But as you can
plainly see, *they* are not here. They laughed and
then promptly left, making lame excuses."

"Well, I'm sure we can figure this out," Leo
said.

His optimism, Piper thought, *is one of his more
maddening traits.*

A third crash sounded from downstairs and

Piper crossed her arms and glared at Leo as she contemplated freezing him, too.

"Why don't we go back downstairs?" he suggested.

"Fine," she said, crossing to the door and flinging it open. She unfroze the children before Leo could ask her what had happened.

"Pwiper, where's my mommy?" a little girl with a cherubic face asked.

"What's your name?" Piper asked.

"Tammy Reynolds."

"Darryl, you got a Tammy Reynolds in your stack of pictures?" Piper called downstairs.

"No," Darryl yelled. "Sorry."

"Reynolds. Well, that's a start. What's your mommy's first name?"

"Mommy."

Piper slapped her hand against her forehead and groaned. Leo put his arm around her shoulder.

"What does your daddy call your mommy?" Leo asked.

Good thinking, Piper thought.

"Baby."

"Ah, I see," Leo said, frowning slightly. "And what does your mommy call your daddy?"

"Honeybunch."

"So much for that," Piper said.

"Well, maybe we can check for Reynolds in the phone book."

"Yeah, that's provided they're even listed.

Besides, there's like over a hundred people with the last name of Reynolds in the city."

"How would you know that?" Leo asked.

Piper waved her hand dismissively. "When I was eight we tried to find the phone number for this boy Prue had a crush on. Come on, hopefully Darryl knows who she is."

Piper addressed the small band of children. "All right, everyone downstairs, pronto. March."

The children turned obediently and like little soldiers marched down the stairs. Leo took advantage of their averted eyes and orbed out before Piper could protest.

"He's the one who wants kids," she grumbled. "He should be the one who has to be here taking care of them."

Sitting in her seat waiting for the concert to begin, Paige had an unexpected reaction. The sights and sounds brought her childhood rushing back to her, and she found herself weeping quietly.

Finally she looked upward and whispered, "I love you, Mom and Dad."

She felt a wave of warmth wash over her and she couldn't help but smile. Dashing away her tears as the lights dimmed, she wondered, *Who says you can never go home again?*

As the orchestra played, Paige slid down into her seat and sat with her eyes closed, letting the music soothe and comfort her.

There was a pause, and suddenly a new sound filled the air, sweet and haunting. Paige opened her eyes. A man was standing, playing a flute solo. The music called to something inside her and she sat up abruptly, leaning forward.

The man played with such passion that Paige felt her heart begin to pound in response. Her breath came in great gasps and she pressed her hand against her breast.

Too soon his solo was over and he took his seat as the rest of the musicians started up again. Paige slumped back in her seat, dizzy and out of breath. *Wow!* she thought.

Intermission came quickly and Paige took the opportunity to peruse the program more closely. The flutist's name was Dale Allen and he had played with orchestras all over the world. She noted with a thrill that he had another solo coming up after intermission.

The lights dimmed briefly, signaling patrons to return to their seats. Paige closed her program and waited with bated breath for the performance to continue.

When Dale Allen stood for his second solo, Paige was more entranced than during the first. She had a nearly overwhelming urge to leave her seat and run to him, to be closer to the music and to the man who played it.

But then—perhaps fortunately—the solo ended, and once again she slumped back in her seat, exhilarated and disappointed all at the same time.

I'm going to have to come back again, she thought feverishly.

As soon as the performance was over Paige tried to get tickets for the next night. It was sold out already, but she was able to procure a ticket for Saturday. Satisfied, she headed home.

As Piper walked down the stairs a little boy tugged earnestly on her sleeve. "I have to go to my piano lesson," he told her solemnly.

"Do you know the name of your teacher?" she asked through tight lips.

"No."

"Then you're going to have to miss your lesson."

She made it all the way downstairs and into the living room, where she stopped dead in her tracks.

Six children—and twice as many stuffed animals—were sitting in a circle, with all her best dishes scattered between them.

"What is going on here?" Piper asked.

"We're having a teddy bear picnic," one little girl informed her, holding up one of the cuddly guests.

"I have to go to my piano lesson," the boy repeated, starting to cry.

"I told you, we don't know who your teacher is," Piper said through gritted teeth. "We don't even know who your parents are," she added under her breath.

"He has the same piano teacher that I do," Tammy spoke up. "Mrs. Culp. She thinks I should cut my fingernails, but I don't want to."

"Aha," Piper said. "You don't happen to know his name, do you?"

"He's Jared Williams. He lives across the street from me."

Piper blinked, unwilling to believe her good fortune. She knelt before the girl. "And do you know your address?"

"Yes, my phone number, too!"

Piper felt like shouting for joy. Finally she had gotten a break. She grabbed the girl's hand. "Then let's go call your mommy."

The Reynolds and the Williams families all arrived within fifteen minutes. They grabbed their children, weeping over them and scolding them at the same time. After a minute, Piper interrupted.

"Excuse me . . . you don't happen to know who any of these other kids are, do you?"

All the adults shook their heads. "Sorry," Jared's father said. Within a minute they were gone, taking two of Piper's problems with them.

"Darryl, how many of these children do you have information on?" Piper asked.

"Ah, let me check," he said, digging a stack of photos out of his pocket.

He sorted through the photos quickly and then looked at her. "Six of them."

"That's it?" Piper asked in despair.

"So far. That might have changed in the last couple of hours."

"Fine, you take those six to the police station. Contact their parents and find out if any others have been reported missing since you left. Then get back here and help me out."

"I don't have any child seats in my car," he protested.

"Darryl, I think this qualifies as a police emergency, don't you?"

He stared at the sea of faces. "Right. I'll drive slow and put on the siren."

"I'm sure the kids will love that," she told him.

Minutes later Darryl departed with his six, leaving Piper with twelve.

"Okay," Piper yelled, loud enough for all the remaining kids to hear her. "Who here knows their phone number or address?"

Six raised their hands. *Okay, progress,* she thought. "Into the kitchen then, we've got some calls to make."

An hour later Piper only had six children left, and they were all hungry. Piper tied her hair back into a ponytail and rolled up her sleeves. She fixed peanut butter and jelly sandwiches for everyone, including herself.

Then she sat at the dining-room table with the children, four boys and two girls. Looking at one of the girls, she asked, "Where are you from?"

"Chicago," the little girl answered proudly.

Piper's jaw dropped. "That's a long way away."

"We're on vacation."

"Are you staying at a hotel?"

"Yes."

"Which one?" Piper asked, excitement beginning to grip her.

"Don't know."

Piper's heart fell. Before she could question the girl further, the telephone rang. She rushed to get it amid cries of "Phone! Phone!" from her little guests.

It was Darryl. "Please give me some good news," she begged.

"The parents picked up all the kids I took from the house. Four others have been reported missing, three boys and a girl."

"That's it?" Piper asked in despair.

"Sorry. I'll be right over with pictures."

Piper hung up and returned to the children.

True to his word, Darryl was soon back at the Manor. He walked in and instantly recognized four of the children from their photos, including the girl from Chicago.

"Darryl, what am I supposed to do with the other two?" Piper whispered to him.

"I don't know, Piper. I've got to get these four back to the station and I'll see what I can find out."

"You could take *all* of them," she said pointedly.

"Piper, what if we can't find their parents tonight? Something weird is going on and you don't want to be implicated. Anyway, a police station is no place for children. Child Welfare will get involved and the kids will end up spending the night at a children's home. Depending on what exactly has happened, there might even be an investigation into their families. Do you really want to put the kids through all that when they seem perfectly happy here? Besides, you're a witch. Who has a better chance of finding missing parents?"

She couldn't argue with him, which only made her angrier. She waved her hand in the air. "Fine, go. But you owe me, mister."

Darryl picked up the smallest boy and grabbed the hand of the girl from Chicago. "Ready, kids?" he asked, moving toward the door. He shot a sly smile at Piper. "Good luck," he said.

"Thanks," she said, wishing the sarcasm in her tone could stop him dead in his tracks.

Piper closed the door and turned to stare at the boy and girl who remained. The girl appeared to be about four and the boy maybe three years or so older.

"So, what are your names?" she asked them.

"Nicole Wilson."

"Mark Johnson."

"All right. Nicole, Mark, do either of you know your phone number or address?"

Nicole shook her head adamantly.

"We just moved and I keep forgetting," Mark offered. "I know the last four numbers are 3124."

"Okay. How about your parents' first names?" Piper asked, trying to force her voice to be upbeat.

Again Nicole shook her head.

"Sandra and Paul," Mark supplied.

"Great," Piper said. She stood up and grabbed the phone, dialing information. "Yes, San Francisco. Sandra or Paul Johnson. There isn't? Are you sure? Well, can't you check the unlisted numbers for me?" Frustrated, Piper slammed the phone down and forced herself to breathe.

Time to try a different tack, she thought. *Just think.* She slowly sat back down at the table.

"Okay. Nicole, where did you walk here from?"

"The park."

"Do you live close to the park?"

"I don't think so."

"Mark, how about you?"

"From school."

Aha! Now we're getting somewhere! Piper thought. "Do you live near your school?"

"Yes, I walk home every day."

"Yes! Very good. What's your address?"

"I told you, I don't know, I just know how to walk there."

"From school?"

He nodded.

"Where do you go to school? What's the name?"

"I don't know. School," Mark said.

With a sinking feeling of dread in her heart, Piper realized that there were many elementary schools in the city.

"How long did it take you to walk here from school today?"

"Not too long. I walked fast."

That at least narrowed it down. "Okay, let's go on a little trip," Piper said. She led the kids out to her car.

At the fourth elementary school they drove by, Mark finally recognized the buildings.

"This is my school!" he said, bouncing up and down in his seat.

"Okay, which way do you walk?" she asked.

Within three minutes they were pulling up in front of a house in a residential neighborhood. Piper parked and the three of them got out.

"I don't know how I'm going to explain this to your mother," Piper said.

"Oh, they aren't home yet," Mark informed her.

"It's nine o'clock at night!"

"My parents both work late," he said, producing a key from his pocket.

"You mean you walk home by yourself and are here until late at night all alone?" she asked incredulously.

He just shrugged and opened the front door. Piper followed him inside and checked to assure herself that the house was, indeed, empty.

"You should memorize your address," she told him. "Here, let me write it down for you."

A sheepish look crossed his face. "I know my address."

"What?" she asked, incredulous.

He dropped his eyes to the floor. "I liked being at your house, I wasn't ready to come home."

"And your phone number?"

"No, I really do forget that. I mix it up with the old one."

"Mark, that was not a nice thing to do. It was dishonest."

"I know, I'm sorry."

She stood, staring at him, unsure what to say next.

"Okay, you can go now," Mark informed her.

Piper was torn. She didn't want to leave him all alone. Then again, he was used to it, and it would be easier if she didn't have to explain things to his parents. If she just left, they probably would never know that their son hadn't been home all day. *They should know,* her mind nagged at her.

She looked at Nicole and finally decided. "You lock the door after we leave."

"I know," Mark told her with an exaggerated eye roll.

Piper left, waiting to hear the lock turn before she and Nicole walked back to the car. Once they were inside Piper asked, "Now, what about you? Did you lie to me?"

"No," Nicole said solemnly.

"Can you tell me anything that's close to your house?"

"Other houses."

"I see. Any schools, or stores?" Piper prodded.

"No."

"Okay, I guess it's back to the Manor." Piper started the engine and headed home.

When they got there, Phoebe was lounging on the couch in the living room wearing pajamas and reading a magazine.

"My, don't you look cozy," Piper said through gritted teeth.

"My, don't you look crazy," Phoebe countered. "I see you've still got someone with you."

"Yes, Nicole is the last. If you help me find her parents then I won't have to strangle you in your sleep."

"Have you tried scrying for her parents?" Phoebe asked.

"With what?" Piper asked wearily, dropping into a chair. Nicole sat down on the floor next to her and leaned her head against Piper's leg. Piper was too tired to move and let her head fall back against the back of the chair.

"Sweetie, do you have anything of your mommy's?" Phoebe asked, sitting up.

Nicole nodded and pulled a necklace over her head.

"Perfect," Phoebe told her, casting a triumphant look Piper's way.

Piper stuck out her tongue in reply. She sat and watched as Phoebe got out the maps of the city. *Only tonight we're not scrying for evil, we're just scrying for two people who haven't figured out yet that their child has been missing all day. Then again, maybe they are evil*, Piper thought.

"Okay, let's figure out where her parents are," Phoebe said when she had everything set up on the dining-room table.

Piper remained in the chair, exhausted, as Phoebe began to scry, swinging the necklace back and forth over the maps. Half an hour later they had their answer.

"Your parents are in France?" Phoebe asked Nicole.

Piper sat up, disconcerted. "France?"

"I don't know, they went away on vacation," Nicole said.

Piper felt sick. "Who are you staying with?"

"At home, with Nanny. I don't like her."

This is not happening, Piper told herself. *This is so not happening*.

"Do you have anything of hers?" Phoebe asked, walking over to crouch down by Nicole.

"No."

Piper slumped in defeat.

"I have something of Snowball's."

"Who is Snowball?" Phoebe asked.

"My puppy."

"Is he at your house?" Piper asked, finally feeling hopeful.

"Yes."

The little girl pulled a small rubber ball from her pocket and handed it to Piper. It was slightly sticky, but Piper didn't care that it was covered in dog slobber.

"I'm on it," Phoebe said, snatching the ball from Piper's hand and running back to the dining room.

By the time Piper dragged herself from the chair to follow her sister, the ball was resting on a spot on the map.

Twenty minutes later a very frightened young woman opened the door of a very expensive house and grabbed Nicole from Piper.

"Don't ever run off again!" the nanny shrieked.

Eyes wide, Piper tilted her head to the side, her ears ringing from the sound. *No wonder Nicole doesn't like her,* she thought, wincing.

"Don't forget this," Piper said, handing the rubber ball to Nicole. "I think Snowball would miss it."

"Thanks, Piper," Nicole said. "Do you want to meet him?"

"No, we've got to go home now. You be a good girl."

"Where did you find her?" the nanny asked, her eyes accusing.

No, we're not even going there, Piper thought. "I think, right now, if I were you, all I'd be worried about is how you're going to keep your job once Nicole's parents find out that you lost her at the park."

The woman's jaw dropped open, giving Piper a moment of fiendish glee. Without another word, the sisters turned and hurried back to their car.

Chapter

3

At the end of the day, Darryl was a nervous wreck. He had seen to it that all the children he had collected from Piper were safely back with their parents. Normally reunion scenes like the ones he had seen played out all afternoon would have brought him joy. Today, though, he had been too preoccupied with wondering how it had all come about, and what he was going to do about whatever was going on. He had barely even noticed the tears shed by the parents or the waves of the children as they left. There were too many questions left unanswered.

As he turned off the light on his desk and grabbed his coat to leave, he thought, *I don't even know what kind of story I'm going to have to come up with to explain not only why there were so many missing children today, but also how I miraculously found so many of them so quickly.* He walked to his car and unlocked the door.

After buckling his seat belt, he sat for a moment, rubbing his temples. It was hard work being a police detective, but harder work still to have to hide the fact that he sometimes worked with three sister witches. *There are days I wish I didn't know their secret, days I wish I had never met them. Truth is, though, they're part of my life. They're friends as well as allies and I couldn't do some of the things I've done without their help.*

He drove home as quickly as he could. When he walked up to his door he heard laughter inside.

"Dang," he said under his breath. He had completely forgotten that his sister, Estelle, was visiting for a couple of days. He was supposed to have picked her and his nephew up from the airport.

He walked inside with a pained smile on his face. Before he could say a word his wife shot him a reproachful look.

He threw up his hands. "I'm sorry, but you're never going to believe the day I had."

"Bad enough you forgot to pick up your sister?"

"Yes. Estelle, I am so sorry. Look, I'll make it up to everyone tomorrow night. We'll all go out to dinner, anywhere you ladies want."

Estelle laughed and hugged him. "We're going to hold you to that, big brother."

"You'd better," he said, turning to kiss his wife.

He pulled back, but before he could say anything else, something slammed into his kneecap. He shouted and grabbed for his leg.

"Eric! Don't hit your uncle!"

"Yeah, Eric, don't hit your uncle," Darryl reiterated as he knelt down, coming eye to eye with the boy. He hugged him, carefully removing the toy electric guitar from Eric's grasp as he did. As he hugged his own son, Darryl was reminded of the day's events, and was glad neither of the children in his own house had gone missing.

Darryl's dreams that night were intermittent, punctuated by the sound of Eric stomping back and forth between the guest room and the bathroom. *Tough getting used to a new bed, I guess,* he thought. *But it'd be real nice if he'd let me get some sleep before whatever tomorrow has in store for me.*

The next morning, still somewhat weary, he pulled into the police station parking lot, only then remembering the excuses he had forgotten to come up with. But no one asked him anything about the kids, and by midmorning he began to relax. It was then that the telephone rang.

"Darryl, guess what?" Piper asked on the other end of the phone.

"I'm afraid to," he said. "The morning has been going well, too well."

"Three of our little friends are back, and two new ones as well."

Darryl groaned and reached for his coffee mug, wishing like anything that it was filled with something stronger than espresso.

"Maybe if you hurry, you can return them before they're reported missing this time," she said, mocking him.

He stood with a sigh. As he walked to his car he couldn't decide whether he should be glad to know the sisters or curse the day they'd met.

Piper sighed as she hung up the phone. The children, all five of them, were racing up and down the stairs, screaming with excitement. *Why are they doing this to me?*

"Okay, everyone downstairs, now!" she called sternly.

She had managed to line them all up on the couch by the time Darryl arrived. His face was grim as he came in, and she noticed that he hadn't even bothered to knock.

"All right, everyone with me."

"We don't want to go," Mark said grimly.

"Well, you have to," Darryl said. "I'm a police officer, and you should always do what the police tell you."

"My older brother says police beat people up for no reason," a little boy said.

"They don't. Well, they shouldn't. They almost

never do." Darryl floundered to a halt. "Just get in the car, will you?"

"But I'm not supposed to talk to strangers," protested a little girl who hadn't been there the day before.

"No, he's not a stranger," Piper broke in. "His name is Darryl, and he is a very nice policeman. He's going to help you find your mommy and daddy."

The little girl still looked unsure. Darryl rolled his eyes and dropped down to one knee. "Listen, did your parents ever tell you to call 911 in an emergency?"

All of the children nodded.

"Well, when you're lost from your parents, it's an emergency and they're going to call 911 when they find out you're missing. When they call 911, the police show up."

"Like you?" the girl asked.

"Just like me. Now, your aunty Piper called me because she knew you had to find your mommies and daddies. So, I'm not a stranger, and your parents will be happy to know you're safe and with me."

That seemed to convince the children, and Piper breathed a secret sigh of relief. The children stood and trooped toward the door, except for Mark.

Mark looked up at her with pleading eyes. "Do I have to go home?"

Something tugged at Piper's heart. Maybe it

was the fact that she knew he would be going home to an empty house and be alone for hours. Before she could stop herself, she said, "Darryl. I'll take Mark home. I know where he lives."

Darryl gave her a quizzical look, then nodded. "Bye, Piper."

"Bye, Piper!" the children in his care called as they walked outside.

"Bye," she said, crossing to the front door and closing it behind them.

"Now, what am I going to do with you?" she asked Mark as she returned to the living room.

He shrugged. "I can entertain myself. I'd just like to stay here for a while."

It was against her better judgment, against everything she had thought and felt the last couple days. There was something in his pleading eyes, though, that softened her.

"Okay. But no going upstairs, and if you want something to eat, don't fix it yourself. Tell me instead."

He nodded earnestly.

She stared at him suspiciously, through narrowed eyes. "Are we clear?"

"Yes."

"Okay, then. The remote is on top of the television." Piper turned and left the room, cursing herself silently.

She spent most of the time upstairs cleaning the bathroom and straightening her bedroom. She checked in on Mark from time to time, walking softly so he wouldn't hear her. He sat quietly, watching television. Each time she went away shaking her head.

After three hours she went up to him. "Okay, Mark. Time to go home."

He looked up at her with pleading eyes. She shook her head. "No, I'm putting my foot down. It's time to go."

"Okay," he said quietly.

She sighed with relief as he walked ahead of her to the door.

"You guys should have been there; I'm telling you, it was amazing. And there was this soloist, a flute player—I have never heard anything so beautiful in my entire life," Paige gushed after dinner, as the sisters relaxed on the living-room sofa.

"I'm glad someone had fun last night," Piper said sarcastically, clearly still sore about being ditched with all the children.

"Sounds like someone's got a little crush on this musician," Phoebe said.

"No, you guys, it's not like that. There's just something special about him, and I feel this amazing connection to him. I don't know how to explain it."

"It's a connection all right—a *love* connection," Phoebe said, smirking.

"Stop," Paige ordered. "The two of you should come with me tomorrow night."

"You're going again?" Phoebe asked disbelievingly. "I had no idea you liked that kind of music."

"I do," Paige answered, feeling defensive. She picked up a pillow and hugged it to her. "I always have. It makes me feel in touch with my own artistic side."

"Does this mean we can expect some painting out of you in the near future?" Piper asked.

"Maybe," Paige said, unable to suppress a smile.

"Good, because we need a new piece of art in the living room," Piper said, looking a little less grumpy.

"Yeah, to replace the one that was sorta ruined the other day," Phoebe said.

"A cityscape might be nice," Piper said.

"Ooh, the city at twilight," Phoebe chimed in.

"You guys, that's not how art works. Well, at least not *my* art. I can't dictate what's going to come out, it just does," Paige said.

"Okay, fine," Piper said.

"Are you okay, Piper?" Paige asked, absently stroking the pillow.

"She still has child problems," Phoebe said.

"Still? I thought you got all the rug rats home yesterday."

"Yes, but today, while you were out, two new ones showed up, and I had three repeaters," Piper said, hugging herself.

"You're turning into a regular Pied Piper,"

Paige quipped. "Whoever thought you'd be a baby magnet?"

"What's that supposed to mean?" Piper asked.

"Nothing," Paige answered, rolling her eyes. "I just was never even sure if you were going to have kids."

Piper glared at Paige. "What?" Paige asked.

"Leo wants kids, Piper's not so sure," Phoebe translated.

"How do you know so much?" Paige asked, turning toward Phoebe.

Phoebe leaned forward, lacing her fingers together. "As an advice columnist, I've learned to study what people *don't* say as much as what they *do* say."

Paige lifted an eyebrow.

"Okay, fine," Phoebe admitted, dropping her serious tone. "I asked Leo."

"Phoebe!" Piper exclaimed, throwing a pillow from the couch at her.

"Well, how else is a girl supposed to get the scoop when her sister is being so close-lipped?" Phoebe asked, her best innocent expression firmly in place.

"You mean when I told you that, you already knew?"

Phoebe smiled.

"You know, sometimes I'm really glad I was adopted. If I had grown up here with you two, I'd probably be just as screwed up as you are," Paige teased.

"Hey!" Piper and Phoebe responded in unison.

"See," Paige said, stretching. "You even sound alike. Weird."

"All right," Phoebe said, yawning as she dragged herself to her feet. "As much as I'm enjoying all the sisterly bonding, I have to get some sleep." An impish look crossed her face. "Although if Leo gets his way, Piper might not get much."

"That's it," Piper shouted, leaping to her feet and chasing a screaming Phoebe up the stairs.

Paige slid farther down into the couch and chuckled. It was good to see everyone having a little fun. She thought about what she had said earlier. She was—for the most part—glad that she had been raised by her adoptive parents. They had been wonderful. Deep down, though, she sometimes regretted the fact that she hadn't know her sisters when they were younger. She sometimes felt like the odd witch out, and wished she could share all of the stories and inside jokes that Piper and Phoebe did.

It's okay, though, she thought. *We're building our own stories and inside jokes. Maybe someday I won't feel like an outsider at all anymore.*

The next morning, Piper had a headache, which was why she was lying on a couch with an icepack on her head when Leo finally decided to show his face.

He came in through the front door, and she could hear his footfalls in the hall. "I don't want to hear your excuse," she told him, more than a little miffed that he hadn't shown up the night before.

"It's a good one," he said.

"I don't care."

"Okay, fine. I am sorry, though. Forgive me?"

"I'll think about it."

"So, how did it go?"

"Don't ask," she said, groaning.

The doorbell rang and she sat bolt upright, her heart beginning to race. "Don't answer that!"

"Why not?" Leo asked, moving toward the door.

"It could be more of them."

"Piper, I don't think you're feeling okay," he called from the hallway, and then Piper heard the door open.

A wide-eyed boy came stumbling in, carrying a baby in his arms.

"No, I'm definitely not feeling okay," Piper hissed. To the boy, she said, "Go home, your mother will be worried."

"I don't know how to get there," the little boy said.

"Great," Piper said. She sank back into the couch and covered her face with her hands.

"Son, why did you come here?" Leo asked, kneeling down next to the children.

"I dunno, I just had to."

"And do you remember the way you came, the path you walked to get here?"

"No. There were too many turns."

Piper let out a little scream of frustration. The boy ran over to her. "It's okay, lady." He thrust the baby into her arms. "Hold Gracie, everyone likes to do that."

"No, wait, I don't want to hold her!" Piper protested. But the boy ignored her and ran over to Leo, who began talking earnestly to him. Piper looked down at Gracie. She had an incredibly beautiful, cherubic face, and Piper softened. "You'd put all those babies in the commercials to shame, wouldn't you?" she asked.

The baby nuzzled closer. Piper looked up to see Leo staring at her, a smile on his face and what looked like tears sparkling in his eyes. *He really wants a child*, she thought.

She smiled back at him. Just then, Gracie bit her on the breast. "Ow!" Piper shrieked.

"What is it? What's wrong?" Leo asked, leaping forward.

"She bit me!" she shouted, holding the baby out at arm's length.

"She's just hungry, lady," the little boy said.

"I don't care what she is—get her away from me!"

"Mary," Paige called, walking into the dress store.

The woman turned around and looked at Paige in astonishment. "Is there something wrong with your dress?"

"No, it was great," Paige assured her, "but I need another, the red one."

"The slutty one?" Mary asked.

"That's it," Paige said, excited until she realized that probably wasn't a good thing. "The one with the slit," she said, motioning to her leg.

"Yes, I know," Mary said with a tight smile. She retrieved the dress, bringing it back to the counter.

"You remember my size?" Paige asked.

"How could I forget? You had me bring you every dress in the store the other day."

"Ah. That's right. Well, thanks," Paige said, forcing a smile across her face.

She paid for the dress, silently apologizing to her credit card, and headed for the door, whistling. *It's going to be a good night. Now I just have to get some shoes to go with this dress. And I think I know right where to get them.*

Phoebe sat, drumming her fingers against her desk. *Why am I having such a problem focusing today?* she wondered. She couldn't find a letter that grabbed her; they all seemed to run together. *Everyone has the same problems, just different packaging,* she realized. She spun slowly in her chair, staring up at the ceiling.

People who love too much, people who love too

little, people who don't even know what love is. She stopped spinning and closed her eyes. *I wonder if Piper has had any more uninvited visitors. I really wasn't as sympathetic as I could have been. I know she and Leo are going through a lot; it's a big decision to have kids. Still, even if she doesn't think so, I know that she's going to be a great mother. I'm not sure I will be, but I hope someday I get the chance to find out.*

A knock snapped her out of her reverie. She sat up and opened her eyes.

"Sorry to interrupt you," said a young guy who Phoebe thought was a new intern.

"It's no problem. Can I help you?"

"Um, there was a call for you a little while ago. The guy said it was urgent." He stood looking uncertainly at her and shifting nervously from foot to foot.

Phoebe waited for him to continue, and when it became apparent that he wasn't going to, she asked, "Did you get his name?"

"No."

Phoebe stared at him disbelievingly. He turned three shades of red under her gaze.

"I did get his phone number," he quavered, inching toward her desk with his arm fully extended, a piece of paper fluttering between his fingertips.

She reached out and took it from him. He jumped back as though he had been bitten.

"Thanks."

"You're welcome," he stammered before skittering away.

Someone's been drinking way too much coffee, Phoebe thought, shaking her head.

She glanced at the number on the piece of paper. It didn't look familiar to her. She picked up her phone and dialed. Four rings later, an answering machine picked up.

"Hi, you've reached 555-3128, leave a message after the beep," a male voice said.

Phoebe waited for the beep, still puzzling over who it could be.

"Hi, this is Phoebe of Ask Phoebe. I'm returning a phone call I received at the office. I'll be here until four. Thanks."

She hung up, frustrated. *Why do people have answering machine messages where they give only the phone number and not their name? Oh well, hopefully my mystery man will call back.*

She picked up another letter and began to read.

Dear Phoebe,

I love my family very much, but I'm having some trouble with my son. He is ten years old and a gifted musician. He doesn't like music, though, and wants to quit playing. I'm worried that he's squandering his talent. I don't want to pressure him, but I want to give him every advantage I can. What should I do?

Sincerely, Mother of Talented Son

The phone rang and she picked it up, letting the letter fall back on her desk. "Hello?"

"Phoebe, come home."

"Piper? Are you okay? What's wrong?" Phoebe asked, heart pounding.

"There are more kids, they keep coming, and one of them bit me."

"I'm sorry, Piper, I sympathize, I really do, but I have to get some work done. I can't just leave unless there's a real emergency."

There was a long silence and then Piper added in a quiet, menacing voice, "Paige is borrowing your red shoes."

Phoebe sat up straighter. "The ones with the three-inch heels?"

"Yes."

"I'll be right there."

"Paige! Take off those shoes!" Phoebe shouted as she entered the house. She stopped short in the living room. "What the—"

Piper was sitting in the middle of the floor, head in her hands. Around her, children pranced in a circle, singing "Ashes, ashes, we all fall down!"

On cue they all tumbled to the floor in a screaming heap. One of them fell against Piper, but she didn't move.

"Creepy, isn't it?" Paige asked behind her.

"What?" Phoebe asked.

"Ring around the rosies. The song is about

death. You know, they all fall down dead because of the plague, and the posies in their pockets are to mask the stench."

"Now that is just so wrong," Phoebe said, turning to her sister.

Paige looked stunning. She wore a long, red gown with a slit up the side. Her hair was swept up on top of her head, with small wisps framing her face. Makeup enhanced her eyes, and her already full, red lips looked extra lush. There was a glow to her that made her a vision of loveliness. And on her feet were Phoebe's red shoes.

"Take off those shoes and no one gets hurt," Phoebe said.

Paige shook her head. "No can do, they go with the dress."

"You are not wearing those shoes."

"Come on, Phoebe. It's just for the night. You won't be wearing them and I don't have any shoes that will go with this. I'll let you borrow the dress sometime."

"You do look great," Phoebe admitted. "And they are the perfect shoes for that dress."

"You won't regret it."

"I'm regretting it already. Go, have fun."

"What are you going to do?" Paige asked.

Phoebe turned back toward the living room. "Help Piper, I guess."

Paige snorted. "Good luck. I tried. Those kids just don't stop."

"Great. Just great," Phoebe said, staring at

Piper. Behind her she heard the door slam as Paige left for the symphony. "Cinderella's off to the ball and I'm stuck with the ashes."

Paige sat in her front-row seat, wearing her new red dress and her borrowed heels. Phoebe had nearly changed her mind at the last second when Paige had gone back to get her shawl. God forbid anything happened to the shoes—it would take a week of Paige's salary to replace them. *Why is Phoebe so possessive about her shoes, anyway?* she thought.

No matter. She—and Phoebe's shoes—were comfortably settled. The house lights flashed their warning and Paige's excitement grew.

When Dale came onstage she could see him clearly. For just a moment she thought his eyes met hers. She smiled, but his gaze slid away and she wasn't sure if he really had been looking at her.

The music was more entrancing than she remembered. She had begun to believe that she had built it up in her mind. Now she realized that her memories had not done it justice.

The music washed over and through her, making her feel tinglingly alive. It felt as though her mind and heart began to open and tiny flashes of inspiration went off like fireworks. Spells chased each other through her mind, one on the heels of another.

When the concert concluded Paige began to

cry, overcome with emotions, some of which she had never felt before. After everyone else had gone, an usher came.

Without saying a word, he helped her to her feet and got her outside. He hailed a cab and opened the door for her.

"Where do you live, miss?" he asked.

She told him and he instructed the cab driver. Grateful, she sat back in the seat and closed her eyes, trying to get control of herself.

Chapter

4

Leo was having a bad day. No, *terrible* was a better description, he realized. The Elders had no idea why children were being attracted to Piper. That didn't make him happy. Worse, it made Piper angry, which made Leo even more unhappy.

Then he'd had to spend the day watching over a new charge—a medical intern in an emergency room. The woman, Sandra, was just discovering the extent of her powers, and the temptation for her to help her patients by using them was nearly overwhelming.

Leo understood. When he was alive he had been studying to be a doctor, and it killed him to have to stand by now and watch people coming into the emergency room that he couldn't help. But he couldn't interfere.

Earlier, a patient had died on the table, and

Sandra was taking it hard. Leo could feel her pain, hear her silent pleas for help, and he wished there was something more he could do. *I can't help my wife. How I can hope to help a stranger?* he wondered bitterly.

"Come on, we've got another one," a nurse called to Sandra.

Leo turned to see an accident victim being rushed into the emergency room. He could tell from ten feet away that the man wasn't going to make it. He closed his eyes for a moment, fighting back the frustration of not being able to use his power to heal the man, but he knew from experience that you couldn't fight this kind of injury.

Temporarily childless, Piper left P3 through a back exit, locking the door behind her. She turned and began to walk down the street, feeling grateful that, in a stroke of luck, Darryl had been able to account for all the kids at her house, leaving her with time to herself for the first time in what felt like a week.

An old man was walking toward her. Stopping in front of her, he said, "Piper Halliwell?"

"Yes," she said, gazing curiously at the old man.

He was well-dressed, wearing a button-down white shirt, a vest, and dark slacks. His knobby fingers were wrapped around the head of a sturdy cherrywood cane.

He smiled at her and his eyes held a far-off look, as though he were reliving a special memory.

"Can I help you?" she asked finally.

"You have already helped me immeasurably, and I am very grateful. I can tell that I was right in choosing you."

"I'm sorry, but I don't understand what you're talking about," she said. "Are you all right?"

He smiled. "Better than could be expected."

"Okay, well, I have to go now," she said, backing up slowly. The guy was starting to freak her out.

He thumped his cane on the ground and she glanced down involuntarily. His left foot was twisted to the side, and his shoe could not hide the fact that the foot was crippled and deformed.

"They come to you instead of him," he said. "You can protect them; you are a powerful witch and a compassionate one."

"Who are you?" she asked.

He just smiled. "Keep them safe," he whispered. Then in the bat of an eye, he was gone.

Piper stood, stunned. He hadn't orbed or blinked. *He just disappeared. How, and why? Who is he, and why does he know who I am? What does he want from me?*

Shaken, she turned, but the man was nowhere to be seen. "Hello? Where did you go? This isn't funny!" she called.

There was no answer.

She shivered and began walking again, twice as fast.

After a few blocks she was able to refocus. Her destination was Chinatown, where she needed to pick up a few herbs. The battle with the last demon had diminished some of their supplies.

By the time she made it to Chinatown she had calmed down. She ducked into the herb shop she favored and picked out what she needed. As she was paying for the herbs, she heard a tittering sound coming from the door to the shop.

She turned, suddenly full of dread, and saw a little girl standing there, clutching the hand of her younger brother and giggling. *No, please no,* Piper thought desperately.

She grabbed her change from the stunned cashier and dashed for the door, the children scurrying to get out of her way. *I have to get out of here,* she thought frantically.

She headed up the street, back the way she had come. Glancing over her shoulder she saw the two kids running after her, their mouths gaping in laughter.

She turned and began to run, glancing over her shoulder to make sure she was putting distance between herself and the children. Suddenly, though, just when she thought she would lose them, she caught her foot on an uneven bit of pavement and fell headlong.

She lay still for a moment, hoping nothing was broken. She lifted her head slowly and saw a small wide-eyed boy, standing three feet from her, staring. He began to cry, and turned and ran down the street, shouting for his mother. Piper blinked in amazement. *He left, all by himself! Why didn't he stay with me?*

The pounding of tiny feet interrupted her thoughts and small hands began grabbing at her legs. She leapt to her feet and turned to see the two who had been chasing her. Another girl came running up, clapping her hands excitedly.

"Leave me alone!" Piper said, wishing she could freeze them and escape. There were too many people on the street, though. She couldn't risk exposure. She pushed herself to her feet and kept moving. But the faster she moved, the faster the children ran, and the faster their parents chased them.

It was like Chinese New Year. The small parade of children, with Piper in the lead and confused parents lagging behind, wound through the streets in a serpentine fashion. Cars stopped, people stared, cameras flashed. Piper wanted to cry. The harder she tried to get away, the worse it got.

At last she made it out of Chinatown. By the time she got home she had stopped shaking. Something was still bothering her, though: the memory of the boy who had run away from her.

Maybe it's not all children. If only I could test it

somehow. An idea occurred to her, and she loaded a plate with some of the cookies she had baked the night before. She took a deep breath and headed for Bonnie's house.

"Piper, hi. Do you want to borrow the car seat again?" Bonnie asked as she opened the door.

Piper forced herself to smile. "No, I just wanted to thank you again for the other day. I brought you some cookies."

"Oh, that's sweet. Won't you come in?"

"I'd love to," Piper said.

She followed Bonnie into her house and found herself in the kitchen. They sat at the kitchen table and Piper put the plate of cookies down. "Would your little girl like a cookie?" she asked.

"I don't let her eat sweets," Bonnie said.

"Oh," Piper said. "More for you."

"Yes, they look delicious."

There was a minute of awkward silence. Finally Piper stood up. "I really should go. Is she here? I'd love to thank her for sharing her car seat," Piper said with a wink.

"Oh, I'm sorry. My parents took her to the zoo today."

"Then I'll thank her another time," Piper said. It sounded lame, even to her.

Bonnie reached out and grabbed her hand. "You should definitely have a child."

"Wh-what does that mean?" Piper asked, trying to keep up her smile.

"It's so obvious you want a baby. You baby-sit your cousin's kids, want to see my daughter. It's okay to admit that your clock is ticking. Go ahead, have a baby. You won't be sorry."

Piper backed toward the door. "Uh, thanks for that. Yeah. I'll think about what you said. I'll see you later."

"Feel free to stop by anytime," Bonnie said with a huge smile on her face.

Piper ran back to her house, Bonnie's words chasing her all the way there. Once inside she slammed the door and locked it.

"No children, no children," she said, panting.

"Nope, just me," Mark said, popping his head out from the living room.

She screamed and jumped. "What are you doing here?" she demanded.

He shrugged. "I don't know. It just seemed like the place to be." He turned and went back into the living room.

Piper followed him. "No, really, what are you doing here?"

"Like I said, I don't know. I just felt like I should come here."

"Well, you can't stay."

"Why not? My mom and dad won't get home for hours."

"Because it's not right. Your parents don't know where you are, they don't know me, and besides, I didn't invite you."

"Yes you did," he insisted.

"When?" she asked, trying to keep the anger from her voice.

For the first time the boy's face registered uncertainty. "I thought you did. Someone did," he said.

"I'm not sure I understand," she said, sitting beside him.

"Understanding is not always required," he said, sounding very old and grown-up.

"Something your parents say?" Piper guessed.

Mark got a far-off look in his eyes. "No, it's just something I know. There are things . . . You can't always explain them, but you just know when a thing is right."

What on earth is he talking about? she wondered. She looked at him for a long minute and he gazed back at her guilelessly. *Why is this happening to me? And why now, when Leo and I have been talking about having kids. Maybe it's true, speak of the devil—*

The doorbell rang and Piper groaned. *And they appear,* she thought bitterly. "More of your little friends?"

"I don't have any friends."

A sudden sadness swept her. "It's not good to be alone," she said quietly.

"Just because one doesn't have friends doesn't mean they are alone," Mark answered. The doorbell rang again. "You should get that," he told her.

What a strange child, Piper thought, crossing to

the door. *I wonder what is wrong with him, what his world is like that he can say the things he does?*

Two girls stood on her doorstep.

"Gee, what a big surprise," she said, voice dripping with sarcasm. She opened the door wide and the girls tripped over each other coming in. The girls ran into the living room and jumped up and down on the couch.

Piper chased after them, a warning to get off the furniture dying on her lips. Instead she just stared at Mark, who in turn was staring at the girls. There was something detached about him, as though he was in a different world.

Chapter

5

Phoebe was worried. Both of her sisters were going through something strange and she didn't know how to help them. She sighed and picked up a letter from her desk and then dropped it again.

Piper's problems with the children were rapidly becoming less humorous and more troublesome.

What Phoebe didn't understand was why Piper was attracting children. *Stranger still, it doesn't seem to be all children,* she thought. Piper had told her about the boy in Chinatown who ran away from her. *I wonder if the children who are following Piper have something in common with each other, or with her?* It was an intriguing thought.

Phoebe leaned back in her chair. Paige's behavior was another thing that needed explaining.

When she came home from the symphony she was more excited than Phoebe had ever seen her about anything. The last two days, though, she had become increasingly depressed and moody. It wasn't like her. When things looked bleak Paige was more likely to become angry and proactive, not mopey. Now, though, she was walking around like a ghost, not smiling, barely speaking. It was unnerving.

The phone rang, interrupting her train of thought. Phoebe picked up the receiver.

"Hello?"

"Phoebe?" the man's voice asked.

"Yes, this is she," Phoebe said, trying to sound professional.

"Thank heavens. I need to speak to you."

"Are you the one I've been playing phone tag with?"

"Yes. I need your help."

"I'm listening."

"I can't talk now. I need to see you in person."

"You can come by the paper. I'll be here."

"Seven o'clock?"

"That would be fine." Phoebe's curiosity was getting the better of her. "Do I know you?"

There was a hesitation at the other end of the line. "No, but you helped my brother-in-law once."

The phone went dead and Phoebe sat there for a moment before hanging up the receiver.

• • •

"Okay, so we're right back where we started," Piper said to no one in particular as she surveyed her tiny charges.

Eight children were scattered around the room, and each was playing some sort of instrument. Two of them had real violins and claimed they were practicing for recitals. Some had toy instruments they had brought with them. One boy had turned her pots and pans into an impromptu drum set and was playing them for all he was worth.

The only one who wasn't playing something was Mark. He was sitting in the kitchen ignoring the others. She plopped into a chair opposite him.

"Don't you play an instrument?" she asked at last. "Everyone else seems to."

"I can play any instrument," he said quietly. "I just don't like to."

"Why is that?" she asked curiously.

"I'd rather be practicing other stuff."

"What stuff?"

"I don't know . . . stuff," Mark answered, eyes on the ground.

"I see."

"What's going on down here?" Paige asked, walking into the kitchen wearing her pajamas.

"Paige, I thought you were at work," Piper said in surprise.

"No, I didn't go. I've been in my room. Just didn't feel like going anywhere."

"What is with you? Are you sick?" Piper asked, bewildered.

"No. Can you ask the munchkins to keep it down?"

"I thought you liked music."

Paige winced. "Not their kind." She shuffled back out and Piper stared after her.

"Your sister is depressed," Mark said.

"So it would seem," Piper answered. "Do you know why?"

"No," he said, shaking his head.

"Neither do I," Piper said glumly. She stood up. "I've got to go conduct the chaos."

"Good luck with that," he said with a small smirk.

Without thinking she reached out and touseled his hair. "Little brat," she muttered under her breath.

He smiled at her and she turned away before he could catch her smiling back at him.

Back in the living room she was startled to find Leo sitting on the couch, covered with kids. They were sitting intently, looking at him with big, adoring eyes as he told them a story. Leo had a look of joy on his face that tugged at Piper's heart. After a moment, he looked up and saw her and she steeled herself.

"Animals and children?" she asked, raising an eyebrow.

"Animals and children," Leo confirmed with an angelic smile.

"Busy picturing yourself the head of a big brood?"

"No, just one or two."

"So you say now. I can't believe you've gotten them all to sit still."

"Really, Piper, it's not that difficult. I don't see how they're giving you so much trouble."

"Uh-huh," she said, setting her jaw.

"Come on, they're kids. Innocent, impressionable."

"I'm not so sure about the innocent part," Piper said as one of the girls stuck her tongue out at her. "Don't figure you'd like to stick around and actually help me out this time, would you?"

"Gee, Piper, I'd love to, but I really can't."

"Big surprise there. He runs at the first sign of work."

"Piper, that's not fair. You know I have things to do."

"No, I don't actually know that, Leo. For all I know, when you go off you're playing pool with the Elders."

"The Elders don't play pool, Piper. And neither do I."

"You know what I mean, Leo."

"You're just going to have to trust me, like you always do. I'm sorry I can't be here right now, when you need me." He stood up and moved closer. "Come on, Piper, let's not do this in front of the kids," he said, dropping his voice.

"Why not? Your fan club might as well know who you really are."

"Piper," Leo said warningly.

"No, go if you're going to go. After all, life as we know it might end if you had to stay here."

Piper knew her husband well enough that she could tell he was fuming. He didn't say anything, though, just crossed his arms across his chest. *Maybe I'm a little hard on him*, she thought to herself. *He does spend more time with me than he should, given all his other responsibilities. Still, I get tired of him leaving when I'm in crisis. Unless there's obvious demonic danger, he just assumes I can handle anything and everything by myself.*

"I really do have to go," he said at last.

"Who's stopping you?" she asked, unable to control her sarcasm.

He turned and stormed out the door.

"What just happened?" a little girl asked.

"Aunt Piper and Uncle Leo are getting a divorce," one boy announced seriously.

Several of the children immediately burst into tears.

"Hey, who said anything about divorce? We are not getting a divorce," Piper said.

One girl grabbed her by the hand. "I love Uncle Leo, though, and we'll never see him again."

"No, you'll see Uncle Leo again. Wait, what am I saying? He's not your uncle and I'm not your aunt. Now I've got to get you home to your parents."

"I don't want to go home!" someone wailed, which just made the others worse.

"I'm not going to like this, am I?" Darryl asked when he heard Piper's voice on the other end of the line.

"That depends. How many more missing kids do you have?"

"This isn't my week," Darryl groaned. "I don't know. How many you got?"

"Nine, but I know where four of them live."

"Oh, great. Well, when you figure out where the other five live, let me know."

"Darryl! This isn't funny!"

"Tell me about it. If I show up with one more pack of kids, they're going to start investigating *me*. And we both know how bad that would be."

"Fine, Darryl. Figure out a way to help me, though."

He shook his head and rolled his eyes. "I'll see what I can dig up." He hung up the phone and thought long and hard about retirement. *It might not be so bad. Heck, I could get another job, or we could move somewhere. Maybe it will all be for the best.*

The phone rang again. Praying it wasn't Piper, he answered it.

"Darryl!"

"Oh, hi, honey," he greeted his wife, wondering if now would be a good time to bring up the whole retirement thing.

"We've got an emergency."

"What is it?" he asked, panic suddenly coursing through him.

"Eric is missing. He wondered off from us at the store and we can't find him."

"You've checked the store and the parking lot?"

"Yes, everywhere."

A smirk slowly spread across his face. "Relax, honey, I know where he is."

"How?" she wailed.

"Don't ask how. Just calm down. I'll go get him and I'll be home shortly."

He hung up and dialed Piper, who picked up on the third ring.

"Piper, how's it going?" he asked, unable to keep himself from smiling.

"You know how it's going, Darryl. Please tell me you have some good news for me. Ouch! Will you stop that?"

Darryl bit his tongue to keep from laughing. "Well, I might have some good news. It depends really."

"On what?"

"Whether or not you've got a little boy named Eric there."

"There's a little monster named Eric who just hit me in the shin with a guitar," Piper said, sounding exasperated. "Why?"

Darryl couldn't hold it in any longer. He laughed out loud. "That's the one. He's my sister's kid."

"You're his uncle?"

"Yeah, I'll be there right away to pick him up."

He hung up and wiped the tears from his eyes. *I could just leave him there for a while*, he thought.

He stood up, got his coat, and headed for the door.

"Darryl! So good of you to make it," Piper hissed as she opened the door.

"Anything for you, Aunty Piper," he said in a syrupy sweet voice, punctuating it with a kiss on the cheek.

"Great, thank you. Just what I needed." She swung at him, but he stepped back and her fist only connected with air.

"Where is my little angel of a nephew?" Darryl asked.

"In here," Piper said, leading the way.

"Eric, there's my man!"

"Uncle Darryl!" Eric shouted. He ran up to him and Darryl bent down for a hug. Eric smashed him across the chest instead.

Darryl looked up, his eyes watering. "Adorable, isn't he?"

"Oh yes, that was exactly the word I was thinking of," Piper said smugly.

Eric ran off, chasing three other kids in a circle. Darryl stood slowly, trying to regain his breath. "You didn't by any chance let him have sugar, did you?"

"Oh, you know, maybe just a little bit," Piper said.

Together they watched Eric launch himself off the back of the couch and bounce around the room, ricocheting off kids and furniture.

"Oh yeah, it's going to be a long night," Darryl said.

On days like this Leo felt totally useless. He stood in a mostly empty hallway at the hospital, still fuming over what Piper had said about him running away from work. *I work hard; I do a lot of good. It's just that my job is demanding. I wish Piper could understand that.*

It had been a long day, most of it spent at the hospital watching over Sandra. He was getting worried. He could see her becoming more distressed every day, which was why he was watching over her carefully. After losing a patient, Leo knew Sandra would be questioning her professional choice, and he wanted to be there, supporting her, as much as possible, even though his charges weren't supposed to know who he was or how important he was to their lives.

Just then, Sandra came up behind him and tapped him on the shoulder. "Can I help you, sir?" she said.

Wincing, he turned to face her. "Uh," he said. He usually tried to keep a low profile when watching his charges, but sometimes he blew it.

"I'm sorry, you just look like you could use a

friend. I'm Leo," he said, knowing full well that he probably sounded like a crazy person. Luckily, Sandra smiled and extended her hand.

"I'm Sandra, and you're right," she said. "I need a walk and a talk. But I can't impose on a stranger."

"Who better to impose on? A stranger can't throw anything back at you later," he said.

"Good point," she said. "If you don't mind . . ."

Leo shook his head.

"Great. I don't want to go home and explode at my family," Sandra said.

"Let's grab a cup of coffee," Leo suggested. "In the cafeteria," he added, when Sandra looked a bit nervous at the thought of leaving the premises with a man she didn't know. "And decaf, I think. Seems like you're in danger of spontaneous combustion." Sandra laughed.

Five minutes later they were in the hospital cafeteria, sitting quietly with their cups of steaming coffee.

"So, what's wrong?" Leo asked at last.

"I don't know. I'm worried that I'm getting burned out."

"Maybe you need to take some time off, get away for a couple of days."

"Unfortunately, I think that would be like putting a Band-Aid on a gunshot wound. No, the problem is deeper than that. I work long hours, I barely see my family. I'm not sure if I can keep this up."

"You're going to get through this, Sandra. You've just got to hang in there. Sooner or later things will calm down and begin to make sense."

She laughed. "You almost sound like you understand. There's just so many pressures on me right now. There's a lot going on in my life. Some of it's new, hard to get used to."

Leo was listening, but his eyes were on a baby playing on his mother's lap at the next table. He wished he and Piper could come to an agreement on kids. More than that, he wished he could help her with her current problem. "Have you thought about telling them that you're a witch?" he asked.

Horrified, he realized what he had done even before he heard her gasp. He thought about pounding his head into the table, but decided against it. Looking up at her, he said, "I'm sorry, Sandra, I shouldn't have said anything."

She was white as a sheet and shaking. "How did you know?" she asked.

"I just know. I've been worried about you."

"Me, too." She was beginning to cry. "My husband knows. I told him everything as soon as I knew what was happening to me."

"Maybe you just need some time away from work, to get everything sorted out and to reconnect with each other."

"You're probably right." She stood quickly. "I'm going to go home right now and talk to him about it." Her face softened. "Thank you. I don't know how you showed up at the exact moment you did, and how you know what you know, but thank you. You're an angel." She turned and left.

Leo sat back with a sigh. "More than you know," he said under his breath.

Chapter

6

It was half past ten when Phoebe gave up waiting for her mystery caller. "I guess it couldn't have been that important if he didn't show up and couldn't be bothered to call," she said as she left her office.

What if something prevented him from coming? The thought nagged at her as she passed by the janitor, the only person besides her left in the building.

She opened the front door and stepped outside. Something was wrong; she could feel it. The hair on the back of her neck was standing on end.

As she reached her car she heard footsteps behind her in the dark. Spinning around, she said, "All right. Whoever you are, you have no idea who you're messing with."

"Phoebe Halliwell?" a man in a black trench coat quavered.

Okay, so you do know who you're messing with, she thought. "What do you want?" she asked.

"Help," he gasped, taking a step forward.

"Huh?" she asked.

He began to fall forward and she rushed to catch him. She looked into his eyes and realized that something was terribly wrong. "He's killing, you have to stop him," the man pleaded.

"Who, who's killing?" Phoebe demanded.

"Don't . . . let . . . him . . ."

The man's faltering words came to a stop and she feared that he was dead.

"Leo!" she shouted.

"Phoebe?" Leo asked as he orbed in. He was wrapped in a bedsheet. *Ooops!* Phoebe thought. *No time for embarrassment, though.*

"Help him!" she cried.

Leo bent down and passed his hands over the man's body. Nothing happened and after a minute he stood up.

"What's wrong?" Phoebe asked.

"I can't heal him. He's dead, Phoebes. Do you know how long ago he was stabbed?"

Phoebe glanced down and for the first time noticed that the front of the man's shirt was blood-soaked. Tears stung her eyes as she lowered him gently to the ground and stood up.

"He, uh, he asked me to help him. Said someone was killing people."

"Who?" Leo asked.

"He didn't say." Phoebe bit her lip and turned

her head away. She hated to lose an Innocent. It tore into her gut and she felt sick inside.

"Well, it looks like a job for the police, not witches," Leo said gently.

Phoebe nodded slowly and pulled out her cell phone. "I'll call Darryl."

"Do you need me to stay with you?" Leo asked, wrapping his sheet a little tighter around himself.

She shook her head, barely holding back the tears. "No, go back to Piper; she probably needs you more than I do right now."

Leo stared at her piercingly, but Phoebe didn't flinch. "Okay," he said, sounding resigned. "Call if you need anything."

He orbed out before she could even thank him.

Phoebe hit the speed dial for Darryl's cell and stared down at the dead man. *He knew my name. Why would he come to me for help unless it was something magical? I'm not the police or even a reporter. There would be no logical reason for him to come to me unless he knew who I was or what I could do. If that's the case then there must be something demonic at work here.*

"Hello," Darryl answered.

"It's Phoebe. Can you come to my office?"

"If this in any way has to do with kids, the answer is no," he said emphatically.

"No, no kids." She took a deep breath. "A man's been murdered." She hung up before he could reply. "Who were you?" she asked the body.

It seemed like only a couple of minutes before Darryl arrived, along with a half dozen other police.

"I'm sorry for disturbing you at home," Phoebe said.

"Don't worry about it, my nephew was refusing to go to bed and it was getting ugly there anyway."

"Huh?"

He waved his hand. "Forget it. What happened here?"

"This guy's been trying to reach me for a couple days; I'm not sure why. He was supposed to come by earlier tonight, but he never showed. When I finally decided to head home, he was here. He died before he could really say anything."

"Do you know who he was?"

She shook her head. "Not even his name, isn't that pathetic? A man died trying to meet with me and I don't even know who he was."

"It's not pathetic. For all we know he's some wacko stalker."

"No, I don't think so," Phoebe said, dashing the tears from her eyes. "He sounded like he was in trouble, like he needed help. I failed him."

Darryl pulled her a few steps away and lowered his voice. "Look, you didn't fail him, all right? Now, I need you to pull yourself together, understand?"

She nodded.

"Okay. I got your statement, you get out of here. Go home. I'll call you when I got something."

"Okay."

"Do you need me to get someone to give you a ride?"

"No, I got it. Thanks, Darryl."

"You're welcome," he said. "Now go."

Phoebe was shaking when she reached the Manor. She had seen death before and it was always horrible. What made it worse was that she had lost an Innocent, one who had been coming to her for help. *And he wasn't even killed by supernatural means. What could he have possibly thought I could help with?*

She could hear Paige banging around in the kitchen, which just made Phoebe feel worse. Piper was up, sitting on the couch and looking very tired and quiet.

Phoebe sank onto the couch next to her and leaned her head on Piper's shoulder. They sat there for several minutes, staring off into space.

"You're home late," Piper said, breaking the silence.

"A guy wanted to meet me, said he needed help. He was three and a half hours late and had a gaping chest wound when he got there. Died before he could tell me what he wanted to see me about."

Normally Piper would have reacted strongly, putting her arms around Phoebe, expressing her horror and concern. Tonight was different, though. They sat in silence for another minute before Piper finally said, "That sucks."

"Yeah. Sorry I pulled Leo out in the middle of . . ."

"It's okay. All we were doing was debating the merits of birth control."

"Then I'm not that sorry," Phoebe admitted.

Piper kissed the top of her sister's head. "Neither am I."

"His name was Peter Jacovich, and he was a cellist with the San Francisco Symphony," Darryl told Phoebe the next morning.

Phoebe clutched the phone tighter in her hand. "The symphony? Are you sure?"

"Yes, why?"

"Paige has been twice in the last week."

"I stopped believing in coincidences the moment I found out what you girls were," Darryl said.

"Me, too," Phoebe admitted. "Did you find out anything else?"

"Only that he had been stabbed with some kind of long wooden object."

"That's odd."

"Yeah, coroner's still working on it."

"Darryl, could you check something for me?"

"What?" he asked, suspicion in his voice.

"This guy did say one thing. He said that I had helped his brother-in-law."

"Who's his brother-in-law?"

"That's just it, I don't know."

"Ah, so you want me to check it out."

"Yes, please," she said.

Fifteen minutes later Darryl called back. "He only had one sister and she's only been married once. The husband's name is Hadley, Bradley Hadley."

"Is that some kind of joke?" Phoebe asked.

"No joke. I hope this helps." He gave Phoebe the address to Bradley Hadley's house.

"Thanks," Phoebe said, then hung up the phone.

Bradley, Bradley, do I know anyone by that name? Something struck a chord, but she wasn't sure what it was. *Maybe Piper will know,* she thought.

Piper was upstairs, hanging up laundry. She looked serene in a way that scared Phoebe. It wasn't like her. *Nobody's acting like themselves,* Phoebe thought.

"Piper?" Phoebe asked.

"Yes?"

"Are you okay?"

"Why shouldn't I be?" Piper asked.

It was then that Phoebe started backing toward the door. "No reason, just checking. I'll be downstairs."

She turned and fled. The energy coming from

Piper was intense. Phoebe wondered if her sister and Leo had spent the rest of the previous night fighting.

She went into the kitchen and drank a glass of water. As she was putting the glass in the sink, Piper entered the room.

"What did you want, Phoebe?"

"Look, Piper, I know you're not in a good mood."

"Whatever makes you say that?" Piper asked. Her tone was like honey, but her fingers were white where they gripped the edge of the table.

"Yeah. Well, it looks like you don't want to talk about it right now. That's okay. I just need your help."

"Okay."

"Can you remember if we ever helped someone called Bradley?"

"Bradley. That sounds familiar." Piper thought about it for a minute. "Hmmm. Didn't we save a Bradley who was being stalked by an ex-girlfriend who was a demon?"

"That's right!" Phoebe exclaimed. "And he had a wife."

"Yes."

"The wife is the sister of the dead guy from last night."

"Weird. Do you think there's a connection?"

"Well, he knew who I was because of his brother-in-law, but I don't think there's a connection other than that."

"Maybe we should pay Bradley a little visit," Piper said.

Phoebe turned, hearing a loud noise on the porch. "Looks like I'll be visiting him alone."

"Why?" Piper asked.

The doorbell rang and Phoebe turned back to her. "I'm guessing that's for you."

Phoebe headed out, letting four kids in as she did. She closed the door quickly behind her to block the unladylike noises being made by Piper.

It took her twenty minutes to get to Bradley's house. When she got there, though, a young woman told Phoebe that she was house-sitting and the Hadleys wouldn't be home for another week. She had been instructed not to give their phone number to anyone. Phoebe couldn't persuade her otherwise, so she finally gave up and drove to the office. Maybe she could find out something more about the man who had died in her arms.

"You again?" Mary asked, arching her eyebrows.

"Yeah," Paige admitted. "I'm going to need the white dress."

Paige could barely focus on the concert. She was busy thinking of what she was going to say when she met Dale. She planned to wait by the musician's entrance for him, even if it took all night. When he began to play she was able to concentrate, hanging on every note. When he sat down she returned to her rehearsing.

Five minutes before the concert was over Paige got up and left. She hurriedly made her way outside and stood by the exit the musicians would use.

She didn't have long to wait. Dale was one of the first musicians to exit.

"Excuse me," Paige called.

"Yes?" Dale said, turning toward her.

She suddenly felt like a tongue-tied idiot. *Good, Paige, stand here a few more seconds like an idiot, let him think you're a psycho stalker.*

"I just wanted to tell you how much I enjoyed listening to you tonight." *Okay, that at least sounded fairly normal.*

He smiled. "And what about Saturday? Did you not enjoy listening to me then?"

So much for not looking like a stalker. "Yes, of course, you were wonderful."

"Good. I would hate to think I had put in less than my best efforts. Where were you sitting tonight?"

"Six rows back, center."

"You were in the front row last night?"

"You noticed me," she said, feeling herself blush.

"It was a little hard not to."

"Well, the dress was—"

"No, not the dress, your smile. It lit up the room."

From any other guy it would have seemed

like a come-on, but not from Dale. He said it with a quiet confidence and conviction. It was as though he had seen a million smiles and was thus qualified to make an impartial judgment about the quality of Paige's.

"So, what specifically do you enjoy about my performance?" he asked. His smile seemed to tell her that he already knew the answer, but wanted her to express it anyway.

"Your passion and your precision. I know it sounds like a contradiction, but you do everything so perfectly and yet there's nothing mechanical about it. You play with such life, such animation. It's inspiring."

"Thank you," he answered. "I have played for many years and I have learned that it is only when you know all the rules and can duplicate them exactly every time that you truly become free to express yourself."

"Wow, that's really deep," she said, lacking better words. "You're saying that there is freedom in following the rules?"

"The ultimate freedom. The universe itself has an order to it, rules. Try and fight them and you struggle to achieve even a very little. Work with them and you can change the world itself."

Something about his words rang true to Paige. She had spent a great deal of her life fighting the rules—the universe sometimes, or so it felt—and she hadn't made it nearly as far as she would have liked. Indeed, every victory had been hard won. Maybe what he was saying was right. It certainly seemed to work for Dale, anyway.

"Are you going to come back tomorrow?" he asked.

"I hadn't decided."

"Please attend. I will do something special, just for you."

She dropped her eyes to the ground and felt herself grinning like an idiot. "Thank you," she muttered.

"You are most welcome. Now, if you'll excuse me, I must retire for the evening. Until tomorrow."

"Until tomorrow," Paige whispered.

When Paige made it home she found that she had more energy than she had had earlier in the evening. Instead of turning in she found herself in the kitchen. She practiced making potions late into the night. By the time she was ready for bed there were a dozen little vials neatly labeled with their contents.

"Good job, Paige," she told her reflection in the bathroom mirror before she began to brush her teeth. She *had* done a good job. Especially the last potion. It had been perfect. She knew it, felt it in her soul.

Even as she drifted off to sleep she was thinking of the potions. She thought she had a great idea for a new vanquishing one. . . .

Chapter
7

Phoebe yawned as she entered the *Bay Mirror* building. Paige had woken her up in the middle of the night by singing in her sleep. Then in the morning, when Phoebe came downstairs exhausted, Paige had the nerve to be bouncy and cheerful. She had talked nonstop all morning.

As she exited the elevator, Phoebe stifled another yawn. *At least she's acting a lot happier than she has been the last couple days. Even that's spooky, though. She's usually not quite so hyper. Maybe we should switch her to decaf.*

"Phoebe, there's someone waiting for you in your office," the intern— *What's his name again?*— told her.

Great, just what I need when I haven't slept worth a darn. The thought of turning around, going home, and crawling back into bed suddenly held great appeal. She sighed, coming back to reality. "Really?" she asked, wrinkling her nose. "Who?"

"Some guy. He looks kind of strange if you ask me, but he insisted on talking to you, said it was a matter of life or death."

The hair on the back of Phoebe's neck lifted and her scalp tingled. "Well, in that case, I'd better see him," she said, trying to sound calm.

When he had turned away Phoebe raced to her office and practically slammed the door shut behind her. Belatedly she realized that the man waiting for her might not be an Innocent in trouble or someone with news, but could instead be a psycho or a demon.

She turned and stared at the man who was sitting in the chair. He wore a dark trench coat. His blond hair was pulled back into a small ponytail and his face was creased with lines of worry. Nonetheless he still managed to cast her a surprised look.

"You make quite an entrance," he noted.

"Sorry about that. Can I help you?" she asked.

"I certainly hope so," he said standing. "I need your help."

"I'm an advice columnist, so unless you're looking for advice on whether or not to propose to your girlfriend, I think you have the wrong person."

"No, I don't need advice, I need help. *Your* help. I play violin for the San Francisco Symphony."

"If this is about the man who was killed, you should talk to the police."

"No, they can't help me. I think I know what is going on. The man who died came to you for a reason. He knew that you had . . . special powers."

"I know my advice is good, but I wouldn't go that far," Phoebe said, trying to play it cool.

"No," he said impatiently. "Magical powers."

"Ah, I see," Phoebe stammered nervously. "Uh, why don't you and I take a walk?"

"As you wish," he answered.

They hurried from the building without speaking. Once on the street Phoebe turned toward him. "So, why do you think you need my help?"

"There is something very strange happening at the symphony. Someone killed Peter, and I believe that more deaths will follow," the man said.

"What makes you think that?" Phoebe asked.

Instead of answering, the man cocked his head suddenly to the side. Phoebe could hear the sound of music dancing faintly on the breeze. Without a word the man turned and stepped into the street. Stunned, Phoebe watched as a truck hit him and sent his body flying through the air.

She screamed and ran toward his body, cars screeching to a halt around her. She reached him, and even as she bent down she knew it was too late. His eyes were already fixed and staring at something she couldn't see.

She slumped down next to the body. *I've lost another Innocent*, she realized. *And I don't even know why*.

"He just stepped out in front of me," the trucker said as he ran up. "I called for an ambulance."

"It's too late," Phoebe said. "He's gone."

"Oh," was all he could utter. "Oh no."

Phoebe looked up at the driver. "It wasn't your fault. There was nothing you could have done," she said.

"Thank you," he whispered, tears beginning to stream down his face.

Phoebe nodded slowly and looked back toward the body. *But was there something I could have done?* she wondered.

She waited until the police and paramedics had arrived. She told them that the man had stepped out in front of the truck. She purposefully neglected to mention that he had been talking with her just before that.

When she was done she headed home, weary in heart and body. *What would make him suddenly step into the street?* she wondered. *What had he been going to tell me? How can I find out?*

At home she dragged herself upstairs to take a shower, then dressed in a tank top and a pair of sweatpants that hugged her hips.

Downstairs, she wandered into the kitchen

and got herself a glass of water. She wandered into the living room and laid back on the couch, closing her eyes. She hadn't been there for five minutes before she heard the front door open.

"What's up with you?" Paige asked.

"I'm trying to figure out what's going on."

"Why, what happened?"

"Another dead musician."

She opened her eyes and noticed that Paige had gone completely white.

"What did he look like?" she asked.

"He was blond, a violinist."

"Oh, good," Paige said, her voice full of relief.

"Good?" Phoebe asked.

"Well, you know, not good, but I'm just glad it wasn't Dale."

"I'm glad you're relieved, but this is the second guy to die trying to talk to me," Phoebe said.

"That can't be a coincidence," Paige said.

The front door opened and closed.

"I'm thinking not," Phoebe said, sighing.

"What aren't we thinking?" Piper asked as she walked in. She'd just dropped off the last of the wayward kids—again—and she fell into an armchair, looking exhausted.

"There might be something magical at work," Phoebe said.

"Another musician was killed today," Paige added.

"Another one? Where?"

"In front of my office building. He had come

to talk to me. We went for a walk and all of a sudden he stepped out into the street, right in front of a truck."

"Ouch," Piper said.

"Big time," Phoebe replied.

"So what—or who—do we think is at work here?" Piper asked.

"I honestly don't know," Phoebe said.

"Okay, so what *do* we know?" Paige asked.

"Someone's killing musicians from the symphony," Phoebe said.

"Did these musicians have anything in common besides playing for the symphony?" Piper asked.

"I don't know, but at least music is a connection."

"Several of the children that have been following me around seem to have some kind of musical talent," Piper added.

"Can we assume that the two things are related?" Paige asked.

Phoebe didn't look convinced. "Professional musicians and talented children. I mean, I realize that music is a common denominator, but I don't see how they can be connected. Why would these murders be linked to Piper suddenly being a kid magnet?"

"I don't know, but it can't be just coincidence, can it?" Paige asked.

"We don't believe in coincidences," Piper and Phoebe said in unison.

"There you go again, weirdos," Paige said with disgust.

"Are all the children following you musically gifted?" Phoebe asked.

"I don't know," Piper said.

"Well, if any more of them show up, let's see if we can find out."

"Even if they are, what does that mean?" Paige asked. "If only children who like music are following you, what would that prove?"

"I don't know," Piper admitted. "At least it would be something, though."

"So what we *do* know," Phoebe said, sitting up straight, "is that we basically *don't* know anything. Great."

"Time to check the Book of Shadows," Piper said.

"Right behind you," Phoebe and Paige said in unison.

"Weirdos," Piper teased.

Twenty minutes later Paige was still flipping through the Book while her sisters tried other sources of information.

"Wait, I found something!" Paige exclaimed. "No, scratch that, it was *Musi*, not *music*."

"What is a Musi?" Phoebe asked.

"Not what, but who," Paige corrected. "Looks like it's a minor warlock."

"He doesn't like music or children, does he?" Piper asked.

"No luck, he likes frogs and mimes."

"Mimes? We should vanquish him for that," Phoebe said, snickering.

"Moving on," Paige said.

She flipped several more pages before finally slamming the book shut. "I give up, I don't see anything in here that can help us."

"What do we do now?" Phoebe asked. "Call for Leo?"

"He hasn't been much help so far," Piper grumbled.

"Then it's about time he pulls his weight around here," Paige said.

Together the three shouted, "Leo!"

"Don't yell," he said, coming up the stairs. "So what's for dinner?"

"A piping-hot mystery," Phoebe answered. "Another musician was killed trying to talk to me."

"Okay. That's not good."

"That's kinda what we thought," Piper said, wrinkling her nose. "We checked the Book, but there was nothing."

"You think this is linked to the children?" he asked.

"Think, but can't prove," Paige answered.

"Okay, then we need to do some fact finding."

"I can see if I can find any other links between the two musicians," Phoebe offered.

"I can see if Dale knew anything about them," Paige contributed.

"I guess that leaves me stuck with the children. Again," Piper said pointedly. She sighed. "I'll see if I can find out more about them."

When Paige walked into the dress shop, holding her credit card out, Mary already had the green dress in a bag waiting for her. Paige handed Mary her credit card, and Mary handed her the dress. Paige left a minute later with never a word spoken.

She made it home, her mind totally focused on the evening ahead. When she walked in the door, she stopped dead in her tracks. The entire living room was filled with kids, and Piper stood in the middle, towering over them. "Whoa, what is going on here?" Paige asked. "Am I home or at Hogwarts?"

"Very funny," Piper said crossly. "You're at home and we're under siege."

"Well, you said you wanted to find out more about them," Paige said, setting down her shopping bag.

"Right. But not all at once," Piper countered.

"What are we going to do?"

"Do? Nothing. We're waiting for Darryl. He's going to come sort through the kids, and hopefully bring back some info on them after he takes them back home."

"How will he—," Paige began.

"There's a lot of repeaters here," Phoebe chimed in from the sofa. Paige hadn't noticed her earlier because she was half-buried under a pile of children.

"You know, this can't be natural," Paige said. She picked up her bag and started to make her way upstairs.

Piper opened her mouth and closed it three times in rapid succession.

"I think the word you're searching for is *duh*," Phoebe said.

Paige stopped at a flower stand outside the symphony building and on a whim bought a single yellow rose. She brought it to her nose and inhaled its rich fragrance. Then she turned and hurried inside.

An usher asked if she needed help finding her seat, but she told him that she knew where she was going. *A couple more days and I'll have this whole place memorized,* she thought.

She found her seat—orchestra center, six rows back—and settled in. She checked her program and began to reread Dale's biography.

"Ma'am?"

Paige turned to see an usher standing beside her.

"Yes?" she asked, wondering if somehow she had ended up in the wrong seat.

He reached out his hand and she saw that he was holding a white envelope. "I was instructed to give this to you."

She took it hesitantly. "By whom?"

The usher smiled stiffly. "I believe the note will be self-explanatory," he said. Before Paige could question him further he turned and walked away.

Strange, she thought, looking at the envelope. *Who knows I'm here?* A sudden warmth flooded her as she realized who must have sent it. She glanced quickly toward the stage but saw no one.

She opened it and pulled out a thin piece of parchment. On it in gold ink was written, "Enjoy the concert. I will see you afterward."

Excited, Paige began to fan herself with the paper. "Oh, I'm definitely going to enjoy this concert," she said.

"Yes, you will, dear," an elderly woman said with a smile, settling into a seat near Paige.

Paige smiled back before returning her gaze to the stage. She waited anxiously for a few minutes until the house lights dimmed, the crowd became quiet, and the musicians took the stage. As the concertmaster led them through their instrument tuning exercise, Paige sought out Dale's face.

He's staring right at me! she realized with amazement. *How did he know where I would be sitting?*

He smiled and she smiled back, blushing furiously. No one in the audience would be able to tell that he was looking at her, but she felt as though everyone knew anyway. She realized after a minute of blissfully staring at Dale that she was perched on the edge of her seat, and she forced herself to sit back.

Just be cool, she told herself. As the conductor lifted his baton, though, and the moment of complete silence came when everyone held their breath in anticipation, Paige found herself not only breathless, but also overcome with emotion.

By intermission she was in tears. Dale's solo had been more moving than on any other night. The notes had seemed to flow from his flute directly into her soul, igniting a fire there.

When intermission came and the musicians stood, Dale gave her a little bow.

"Yes!" Paige exclaimed.

The old woman reached over and patted her knee. "I knew you'd enjoy it, dear."

Paige turned to her. "It's very . . . stimulating," she said, nodding her head several times and wishing she could think of something better to say.

Standing up, she excused herself and made her way to the bathroom. There she found herself last in line behind fifty other women. She tapped her toe impatiently, receiving an annoyed look from the woman in front of her. Paige thought about tapping louder, but changed her mind, instead drumming her fingers against her arm. She glanced at her watch as the line slowly shuffled forward.

"Come on, come on," she said impatiently, tapping her foot.

Only a few more women had squeezed their way past the line and out of the bathroom by the time the houselights began to flash.

"Unbelievable," Paige muttered. A thought occurred to her and she glanced warily around. She ducked out of line and snuck off to a corner by herself. No one was looking her way. "Well, it is sort of an emergency," she muttered. She glanced around once more and then orbed out—

—and into the bathroom back home. Phoebe, who was taking a bubble bath, screamed. "Paige! What are you doing here?"

"Can't talk, gotta pee. I'll be out of your hair in a second."

"You can't just orb in here like this, Paige," Phoebe said, turning her head away as her sister commandeered the toilet.

"Yes, I can and I did," Paige informed her. "Besides, it was an emergency."

"An emergency?" Phoebe asked.

"Yeah, I didn't want all those people to see me wet my pants."

"Given that you're wearing a dress and not pants, that would be quite a trick," Phoebe said.

"Yeah, well, we specialize in those, don't we? Tricks, magic—anything and everything unnatural that can happen, will. And given that reality, why should I take the chance?"

"Paige, you're impossible," Phoebe chided.

"Nope, just highly improbable," Paige told her as she washed her hands. "Gotta go, bye."

She orbed back into the same dark corner that she had left. The line of women was still there. In fact, it looked as if the line hadn't moved at all. Not surprisingly, though, all the men seemed to be back inside the theater. Paige suppressed a laugh as she saw a couple of women nervously eyeing the men's room. *Go for it, ladies. I'll never tell, and none of us would blame you,* she thought.

Paige hurried back to her seat and settled in, sighing happily, just as the house lights came down and the musicians resumed their places.

Dale ended his second solo with a flourish that she didn't remember, and Paige knew it was for her.

The concert was over far too soon. Paige lingered in her seat while the rest of the patrons made their way out. *Just where am I supposed to meet him?* she wondered. *Maybe out back again.*

At last she stood and made her way slowly into the lobby. He was waiting for her, leaning against a pillar with arms crossed and a smile on his face.

"Did you enjoy the show?" he asked without a greeting.

"Yes," Paige answered, handing him the rose.

"Yellow. For friendship?" he asked, smiling as he twirled the stem between his fingers.

"For beauty, and music," Paige said. His face

fell slightly and she added slyly, "And for friendship."

"Good. You know, generally all great friendships have one thing in common."

"Oh yeah? What's that?"

"Both parties know each others' names," he said pointedly.

"I'm sorry," she said, holding out her hand. "Paige Matthews, your biggest fan."

"Dale Allen, about to be yours," he said. Paige blushed as Dale kept hold of her hand for a moment longer than necessary. At last he released it, and she searched for something to say.

"I've noticed the symphony will only be playing this piece for another week. I guess after that, you'll be going back to wherever it is you came from," she said. Instantly, she regretted it. *Smooth, Paige, really subtle,* she thought, wincing.

He smiled, looking deep into her eyes. "Normally that would be the case. However, there is a chance I'll be staying in the city much longer."

"Really? Why?" Paige asked, trying not to sound too excited.

"The symphony has decided to start up a new program, a children's orchestra, and I'm one of the candidates they're considering for the conductor position."

"Isn't there already a youth orchestra?" Paige asked.

"There is, but it is only open to those age

twelve to twenty. This orchestra will be open to children eleven and younger."

"I see, sort of a Head Start for the musical set?"

"Something like that," he said with a laugh.

"And you'll be the conductor?"

"If everything works out, yes. But there are several others also in the running for the position."

"Well, I can't imagine anyone better qualified," Paige said, flashing him her best smile.

"Let us hope the board agrees with you."

"How can they not? All they have to do is hear you play."

"Really, is that all?" he asked in a teasing voice.

"Well, that, and maybe dinner," Paige suggested coyly.

"And that will guarantee my appointment?" he asked.

"Absolutely."

"Well, in that case, I'd better practice for the big event. Paige, you wouldn't care to accompany me to dinner, would you?"

"Why, I'd be delighted," she answered, flicking him lightly with her wrap.

"Max's Opera Café?" he suggested.

"Sounds perfect."

He smiled and extended his arm. "Shall we walk? I could use the fresh air."

She took his arm and they began to walk the

few blocks. A sense of warmth suffused her and she was amazed at how relaxed she felt. They walked in silence, but it wasn't awkward. It felt very companionable to walk with Dale, as though they were old friends who could just be happy being together.

They arrived at the café quickly, and when they entered the restaurant, Dale received a standing ovation.

Paige blushed and tried to edge away from him, uncomfortable being in his limelight. He held her arm close, though, as he smiled and bowed. Gradually the diners returned to their seats and the maitre d' hurriedly showed them to a cozy table nestled in a corner.

"Wow, I've never been to dinner with a celebrity before," Paige commented after they were seated.

He waved his hand dismissively. "By tomorrow they won't even remember what I look like. I guarantee you half of the people that saw the concert aren't even sure who they were giving the standing ovation to just now."

"That's sad."

He shrugged. "That's life."

"How long have you been playing?"

"All my life."

The waiter came by to take their order. After he left, Dale leaned toward Paige. "I want to hear about you."

She smiled. "Well, I definitely *won't* be forgetting

what you look like. My parents took me to the symphony when I was a child, but I haven't been in years. When I heard you play last week, though, it really touched something in me. You are so amazing. I never knew anyone could play like that. What you said to me last night was a real eye-opener, too."

He shook his head, looking slightly amused. "Paige, you're talking about *me*. I don't want to hear about me or my music. I want to hear about *you*."

"Sorry, I guess you can tell you've had a real impact. Okay, me." She picked up her water and took a sip, noticing that her hand was shaking slightly. *Wow, I can't believe what an effect he's having on me.*

She set down her glass and had a sudden, wild urge to open up completely, tell him *everything*, even about being a witch.

"I, uh, I'm a social worker."

He nodded encouragingly.

"I have two sisters, well, half sisters, but I didn't know that until recently, because I was adopted. They're great, but sometimes I feel left out, you know, because I wasn't there when they were growing up, I wasn't part of the stories. I had another half sister who died before I could meet her. My adoptive parents are dead, my birth mother is dead. I like to paint, but I never have the time because my life is so busy. I have all these new responsibilities living with my sisters. There are things that we do together that take up so much of my time. We help people. We're—"

She bit her tongue to keep from saying *witches*.

"You're what?"

She ached to tell him the truth, and her hands began to shake more. Finally she gasped, "Good Samaritans."

"That's a worthy calling," he said.

She could tell from the way he narrowed his eyes that he knew that wasn't what she had been about to say. He let her get away with it, though.

"Have your sisters come to the symphony with you?" he asked.

"No, I've been trying to get them to, but Piper's had her hands full with all these children and Phoebe's got her hands full trying to find a killer."

"She's a police officer?"

"Um, no," Paige said, wanting to hit herself. "She works for a newspaper."

"She's not 'Ask Phoebe,' is she?"

"Yeah, that's her."

"Several of the musicians read her column before concerts."

"I'll tell her; she'll like that," Paige said.

"What do you like?"

"Besides your music?" She laughed.

"Yes, besides my music."

"I don't know. I like to help people, I like to

dance. I like you," she said, the words coming out before she could stop them.

"I like you, too, Paige."

She was saved from responding by the arrival of the food, which came complete with a singing waiter.

"You know, I've lived all my life in the City and I've never eaten here," Paige admitted after the waiter had finished serenading them.

"That's the nice thing about traveling all over the world," Dale said, leaning in toward Paige. "I get to do all the touristy things and local attractions that so many of the natives miss or take for granted."

"Wow, that must be pretty cool."

He smiled. "It is."

"Won't you find it hard to settle down here if you become the conductor?" she asked.

"I think I could enjoy spending some serious time in San Francisco," he said with a meaning-ful smile. "This city has a lot to recommend it. Besides, maybe you could help me see the sights."

"See the things the natives miss?"

"Yes."

"That sounds great," Paige said, blushing.

Chapter

8

"Are you sure there's nothing in the Book of Shadows?" Phoebe asked from her reclined position on the attic floor.

"Nothing," Piper said, slamming the Book shut.

"There was nothing about music or Symphonies or conductors or kids?"

"You want to look, be my guest," Piper said, dropping down to a seat on the floor.

"Alrighty," Phoebe said, jumping up. She crossed to the book and began to flip the pages.

"I've done that already," Piper reminded her.

"Okay, fine," Phoebe said. She gripped the edges of the book. Taking a deep breath, she said, "Musicians and kids, our problems now. We need to fix them, please tell us how."

The pages of the book fluttered briefly but the book slammed shut. Phoebe's shoulders slumped in defeat.

"Well, I guess that answers *that* question," Piper said tartly.

"We could ask Leo."

"We already did."

"Fine, I guess we'll just have to do this the old-fashioned way," Phoebe said, lifting her chin defiantly.

"And that would be?"

Daniel Thompson was the art critic and resident culture expert at the paper. Phoebe had spent half an hour stalking him through the corridors, constantly arriving everywhere a moment after he had left. His cologne hung in the air, though, and she followed it until she found him next to the break table, a low-fat sesame seed bagel in one hand and a latte in the other.

"Daniel!"

He turned toward her, all shine and flashing jewelry. He smiled coyly at her. "Darling, what can I do for you?"

"I need to pick your brain about the musicians who were killed."

"Oh that, very gauche, such a waste of talent."

"Yes," Phoebe said, forcing herself to smile. "What can you tell me about them?"

"A cellist and a violinist. The cellist had been with the symphony three years and was in a long-term relationship; the violinist eight years, divorced.

"I know that, but I'm looking for something

more. Did they have anything in common?" Phoebe asked.

"Besides you?" Daniel asked flippantly between sips of his double latte.

"What is that supposed to mean?" Phoebe asked, crossing her arms defensively over her chest.

"Come on, sweetie, you were there when both of them died."

She closed her eyes for a moment, trying to calm herself. She opened them back up and glared at Daniel. "Yes, besides me," Phoebe said, making a mental note to turn him into something unnatural one day.

Daniel continued to sip his latte insolently. Finally he tugged on one of his silver-studded earlobes. "Well, I do know one thing. They were both competing for the conductor position for the new children's orchestra."

"Really? Who else is up for that?"

"What do I look like, an information booth? No, you get one free one, sister."

"Actually, you look like a gorgeous man."

"Flattery won't get you anywhere."

"No, it's true. You're a gorgeous man with incredible taste in clothes," Phoebe said.

"Well, you are correct. Okay, here you go. There are two other candidates that I know of, Rudolph Trent and Dale Allen."

"You sure those are the only two?" Phoebe asked.

"That's the scuttlebutt," Daniel told her with a simpering smile.

"Thanks, Daniel, you're the best," Phoebe said quickly, heading off to her office.

"And don't you forget it, missy," he called after her.

Phoebe just shook her head and hurried down the hall.

Leo leaned forward on the living-room couch. "The Elders think there might be some kind of spell at work, at least as far as the children are concerned. They don't know anything about the musicians who were killed by nonmagical means," Leo told Piper.

"Any information on who might have cast the spell, whether it's on me or the kids, or how to break it?" Piper prompted.

"Nothing yet," Leo answered sheepishly.

The front door opened and closed and Phoebe entered the room.

"I take it you found something?" Piper asked.

"I did," Phoebe answered with an impish grin that quickly faded as Paige walked into the room.

"What's going on?" Paige asked.

"I did some research on the two dead guys."

"Anything?"

"I did manage to find out something. The two musicians who were killed were both competing for a conductor position. Apparently there's going to be a new children's orchestra," Phoebe said.

"You guys! We have to do something! Dale is one of the candidates for the conductor position," Paige told them, panic flooding her voice. "We can't let anything happen to him!"

"We won't," Phoebe reassured her.

"Apparently there's one other guy up for the position, Rudolph Trent."

"He must be doing it, he wants the position!" Paige exclaimed.

"Paige, let's not jump to conclusions. We don't know for sure that the conductor thing is more than just coincidence. Whoever this is might just have a thing against string players, or musicians in general," Leo said.

"He's right. Even if the conductor thing isn't a coincidence, we have no proof that it's this Trent person. It could very well be someone else who thinks they'll have a chance if they kill all the current candidates," Phoebe said.

"Okay, then let's watch them both," Paige said. "Just, please let's do something. We can't just stand around and wait for Dale to get killed."

"You really care for him, don't you?" Piper asked, curiosity in her voice.

Paige took a deep breath. "I do, but it's strange. I love listening to him play, I admire and respect him. This connection, it's not like he's just some guy and I have the hots for him. It's deep. To be honest, I haven't even thought about kissing him."

"Wow," Phoebe said.

"What?"

"That's just not normal for you."

"No, I guess it isn't," Paige said. "So what are we going to do?"

"All right, I'll go check out this Rudolph Trent, see if he has anything to do with the killings, or if he knows anything."

"I'm going to continue to enjoy the quiet, currently child-free zone right here," Piper said.

"How is that helping?" Phoebe asked.

"It will *help* me to recharge my batteries and think," Piper answered, in a tone that signaled that the conversation was over.

"I'll call Dale," Paige offered. "He might know something. At the very least, we need to protect him."

"Yes, 'we' need to do that," Piper said, exchanging a quick glance with Phoebe.

"Well, at least one of us does," Phoebe said, smiling.

Darryl picked up the phone with a sense of trepidation. "Hello?"

"Darryl, it's Paige."

"Oh no. No kids, no dead guys. I'm full up."

"No, nothing like that. I need you to find out where Dale is."

"Who?" he asked.

"Dale Allen, the fourth musician."

"Fourth musician what? Paige, are you not

making any sense, or have I had too much coffee today?"

"He's one of the musicians trying out for the conductor position, just like the two dead guys. He could be killed. He might be dead already. I can't scry for him since I don't have anything personal of his, and I've been trying to call him for hours and he isn't answering his phone."

"Paige, I don't know where he is."

"You're the police, can't you do something?"

"Officially, no. Not for twenty-four hours."

"But you were looking for the missing kids within hours."

"That's because they were little kids, not grown men. I'm sorry, Paige; if it was up to me, I'd commit the full resources of the San Francisco Police Department to finding this guy for you, but it's not up to me," he said, trying to keep the sarcasm from his voice.

"But, Darryl—"

"No buts. By the way, not that I want to know, but who is number three?"

"What?"

"The third musician, who is he?"

"I don't know, just some guy."

"That's very helpful. 'Some guy.' 'Some guy' isn't dead or missing, too, is he?"

"I don't know. Phoebe's checking on him, I think."

"Ah. Well, when she knows, give me a call. Until then, just wait. He'll show up."

He hung up the phone before she could say anything more. *San Francisco has turned into an insane asylum, and I'm either the director or the chief patient*, he thought. Sighing, he got up to get another cup of coffee.

Paige hung up after speaking with Darryl and immediately debated calling him back. She had been trying for three hours to get hold of Dale, but he wasn't answering his phone. Panic was beginning to set in, even though she knew there were dozens of things he could be doing that would have him away from his phone.

Phoebe was still out, hopefully questioning Mr. Trent. Piper hadn't done so well with her quiet time. There were now several children in the living room, all banging away on things and hurting Paige's ears.

She picked up the phone and dialed again. One ring. Two. Three.

"Hello?" a masculine voice answered.

"Dale! Hi, it's Paige."

"Paige, good to hear from you. How's the painting?"

"On hold for the moment. Look, I need to see you."

"I'd like that very much. I'm free tomorrow night."

"No, I need to see you before that."

"I can't get away before that. I'm tied up with rehearsals and I have to talk to the board regarding my qualifications to conduct the children."

"Please, Dale, it's important."

"It can't wait?" he asked, his voice lightly teasing her.

"No, actually. Um . . . you know those two musicians who were killed?"

"Not personally, but I know *of* them," he said, his voice quickly growing serious.

"We have reason to believe that you're in danger."

"Who's we?" he asked, his voice barely more than a whisper.

"My sisters and I. Look, it's really hard to explain. I just need to see you in person. Can you come here?"

A sudden boom behind her made Paige jump out of her skin. She orbed momentarily before catching herself and orbing back in time to keep the phone from falling to the floor.

"What's that sound?" Dale asked.

"Nothing. My sister's . . . baby-sitting a bunch of kids, and they all seem to love making music."

"Sounds like you're organizing your own orchestra."

Paige smiled. "So, you want to come conduct it?"

He chuckled. "I'd love to."

Paige gave him the address, hung up the phone, and uncrossed her fingers. She turned and walked into the living room. "He's coming," she informed Piper.

"Great," Piper said, her face haggard and her

voice beleaguered. "Maybe he can help me do something with them," she said, indicating the children with a wave of her hand.

"I don't think so, not unless you want him to organize them into a little orchestra," Paige said with raised eyebrows. "Come to think of it, he did offer to conduct. Who's that kid?" she asked, pointing at one that was sitting off by himself.

"Mark. He keeps showing up, day after day," Piper said with a sigh. "Doesn't like music too much."

"Phoebe's been gone awhile," Paige noted.

"Yeah, I hope she's having more luck than I am," Piper said.

"I hope so, for all our sakes," Paige muttered.

Phoebe sat in the Seal Rock Inn Restaurant, waiting for Rudolph Trent to show. He had agreed to meet with her to discuss things. The restaurant was part of a small inn and served good food, but Phoebe wasn't there to eat.

She sipped her coffee and waited. She had chosen a seat facing the door so she could see everyone coming and going. She had been there about ten minutes when a tall man with gray hair entered. His eyes met hers immediately and he walked straight toward her.

"Phoebe Halliwell?"

She nodded. He extended his hand. "I'm Rudolph Trent."

"It's nice to meet you, Mr. Trent," she said,

shaking his hand. His grip was firm and warm and she couldn't help liking him instantly.

"Call me Rudolph. May I sit?"

"Of course, Rudolph."

He took the chair opposite her. The waitress bustled up.

"Coffee, black," Rudolph instructed.

His coffee arrived in a matter of seconds. Phoebe and Rudolph sipped from their mugs and sized each other up. Phoebe was the first to speak. "Rudolph, I understand that you are in the running for a conductor position?"

He leaned forward, his face lighting up. "Yes, I am. It's for the new children's orchestra that's being organized. There are several programs available right now, including an orchestra for older children, but this would recognize and encourage children with musical talent to participate at a younger age."

"Sounds like you have a real passion for it," Phoebe commented.

"I do," he answered. "I have a master's degree in teaching. I love kids and I originally planned on teaching. Then my musical career took off and I just went with that. As much as I love music, I've always kind of regretted the fact that I never pursued teaching. This would give me an opportunity to share the music I love with the kids. I can't think of anything better."

"Wow," Phoebe said. "This really means a lot to you."

"It's everything to me. I'd do anything to help those kids."

"Including murdering the competition?" Phoebe asked pointedly.

The smile disappeared from his face. "No, I would never do that."

"But you said you'd do anything to help the kids."

"I would, and if that meant stepping aside so a better conductor could lead them, I would. This isn't about me, it's about them. And if you brought me here to accuse me of murder, then I'm afraid we're through." Rudolph rose to his feet, eyes flashing with anger.

"Wait," Phoebe said, impulsively reaching out to grab his hand. "Stay, I need to talk to you."

He sat slowly, clearly curious but still suspicious.

"I don't think you killed those two musicians, but I think you can help me figure out who did. I just need you to answer some questions for me."

"If I can help, I will."

"Thank you," Phoebe said.

The waitress came to freshen up their coffees. Once she was gone Phoebe asked, "Did you know either of the men?"

He nodded slowly. "I knew Peter, the cellist. He and I had played in a quartet together several times. He was a nice guy, wonderful musician."

"Did you know the violinist as well?"

Rudolph shook his head. "No, not really."

"Do you think they knew each other?"

He nodded. "Probably. I saw them talking the day Peter was killed."

"What about?"

"I don't know. I do know I saw them looking at your column."

"My column?" Phoebe asked, startled.

He nodded. "That's why I agreed to meet you. I was hoping you could tell me something. It certainly hasn't escaped my attention that there were only four of us trying for the conductor position and now two of us are dead."

Phoebe dropped her eyes to her coffee cup. "I'm sorry," she said. "I know this can't be easy for you."

"It's not," he said, taking a deep breath. "I can't help but wonder if I'm next."

Phoebe took a sip of her coffee. "Do you know anything about Dale Allen?"

"The fourth candidate? I know that he's brilliant, very gifted. He's traveled the world playing. You can get all that from his bio, though. As far as anything specific, personal, no. I really don't know anything about him. He comes to rehearsals, shows up for concerts, plays, and leaves."

"Is there anyone who might have gotten to know him a little better?"

"I've never seen him talking to anyone in the orchestra, although that doesn't mean that he hasn't," Rudolph admitted.

"I see," Phoebe said. "Has anything else strange been going on that you can think of?"

"There was something that Peter said, just before he died, that's been bothering me," Rudolph confessed.

Phoebe leaned forward. "What was that?"

"Just as I showed up for rehearsals one night, almost a week ago, Peter came out of the building, running. He ran right into me and I nearly dropped my case. I asked him what was wrong, but he was hard to understand. He said, 'I can't believe he's here, not again. I have to get proof this time so I can stop him.' He dashed off and I never had a chance to speak with him about it again."

A chill danced up Phoebe's spine. "What do you think he meant by that?"

"I have no idea. I never saw him again. I wish now more than anything that I had."

Chapter
9

"I'm going to go with Paige, to see what's going on with this musician," Phoebe told Piper over the phone.

In the background, Phoebe could hear the band warming up at P3. "Okay," Piper said. "I'm here at the club, just getting things ready, but I should be home soon. Be careful."

"Will do," Phoebe promised. "Got any of your groupies there with you?"

"No, thank heavens. And the plan is to get out of here as soon as possible, so hopefully they won't track me down here."

"Good thinking. Wish me luck."

"Good luck. I'll talk to you later tonight. Love you."

"Love you, too," Phoebe said, and hung up.

She took one final look in the mirror. She was wearing a simple, no-nonsense black dress. It was dressy enough that she wouldn't stand out, but she knew for a fact that she could still fight in it, and even do kicks. Just in case, she was wearing her black flats. They were her most sensible pair of dress shoes. They didn't look great, but hopefully no one would be looking at her feet.

Great, Phoebe, you're worried about how you look. Remember why you're going. Focus, she thought.

She touched up her lipstick and headed downstairs.

After hanging up with Phoebe, Piper turned around to see that Mike, a huge, burly bouncer who could scare anyone, even warlocks, was walking toward her with a grim look on his face.

She winced and thought about hiding. One look at the determined set of his jaw, though, convinced her otherwise. *If I run he'll just chase me,* she realized. *Crap.*

"Mike, can I help you?" Piper asked, finding it hard to smile around her gritted teeth.

"Piper, I just wanted to tell you, there were more than a few little kids at the door, all asking for you."

"Yikes. How many?"

"I don't know, ten?"

"What did you do?" she asked, peering past him to make sure that they hadn't forced their way into the club.

"I told them to go home. Kids can't come in here."

"And that worked?" Piper asked, stunned.

"Yes, ma'am. Just wanted to let you know."

"What's your secret?"

"I just looked at them," he told her.

Studying him, Piper cocked her head to the side. "Looked at them how, exactly?"

He stepped closer to her so that he towered above her. Then he very slowly tilted his head downward and narrowed his eyes. His mouth was set into a hard, angry-looking line.

Piper unconsciously took a step backward. "Effective," she said.

"Yes, ma'am," he answered, backing off.

"Good, great. You go, go and make sure they don't try coming back."

He nodded and then walked off. Piper watched him go, thinking, *I'm so glad I hired him. And I'm so glad he didn't ask me why a gang of rug rats was at a nightclub asking for the owner.*

She shook her head and turned back to her ledger. She picked up the phone again to call in an order for more margarita mix. The band was sounding good as it warmed up. The doors would open in twenty minutes, and with the kiddies out of the way, it was shaping up to be a good night.

"Thought I'd drop by to see how you're doing, Dr. Johnson," Leo said, as Sandra walked toward him, stethoscope hanging around her neck.

"Thank you. It certainly was a long day."

A sudden commotion down the hall drew their attention. Two paramedics were rushing in with a child on a gurney. "We need help here!"

Sandra rushed over. "What do we have?" she asked.

"Chest wound, boy's alive, but barely," a paramedic informed her in rushed tones.

"What caused it?" she asked.

"Don't know. No weapon at the scene. Mother heard him screaming and found him crumpled up."

"I'll take it from here," Sandra said.

The two paramedics nodded and hurried away, their night's work far from done.

Leo looked down and a chill went through him as he realized that the child was one of the ones he had seen at the Manor. The wound looked like someone had put their fist into the little boy's chest.

"We have to get him into surgery right now!" Sandra exclaimed.

Leo reached out and grabbed her hand. "Sandra, I can help this boy, but you need to trust me."

"What . . . what are you talking about?"

He bent close, whispering so that only she would hear. "I know what you are, Sandra. So I know you will understand me when I tell you I can heal him, without medicine."

Sandra's eyes opened wide and she took a step back, her hand flying to her mouth. She nodded once and Leo picked up the boy and ducked into an empty room.

Carrying the injured child, he orbed to the Manor, where he laid the boy down on the couch in the living room. Passing his hands over the boy's chest, he thought, *He's been attacked by a demon*. He concentrated and felt the healing power wash through him and over the boy.

Slowly the wound healed shut. When he was finished the boy coughed and sat up, wide-eyed. "What happened?"

"You're okay," Leo told him gently. "Do you know where you are?"

The boy looked around. "Piper's house."

"That's right."

"Where's Piper?"

"She'll be here soon. Right now I have to go . . . upstairs for a few minutes. Can you sit here, very still, and wait for me?"

The boy nodded solemnly.

"Good boy," Leo said.

He stood and raced up the stairs, stopping once out of the boy's sight. He closed his eyes and listened to the voices, thousands of them, crying, begging for help. As always it hurt to try to shut them out. Tonight, though, Leo was listening for something specific and when he heard it, he orbed.

Leo orbed into an apartment and instantly heard a young woman—the baby-sitter, he assumed—snoring. He looked around frantically until he spotted the small crumpled body of a young girl on the floor in a corner. He crossed to her and placed his hands over the wound in her chest.

The little girl looked up at him with frightened eyes, a death rattle sounding in her throat. "Come on, come on," Leo whispered, trying desperately. Slowly the wound began to heal. When it had fully closed, he scooped the child up in his arms and orbed out.

At the Manor, Leo set the girl down on the couch next to the boy. He was only halfway back up the stairs when, from among the voices, he heard what he needed and orbed out.

A very nervous Phoebe approached the symphony building, struggling to keep up with Paige, who was speed walking, despite her three-inch heels. Phoebe wasn't sure what she was going to find, but she'd had misgivings all day. *There's something going on, something that's not right*, she thought.

She was worried about Paige. Her sister's obsession with the musician was unlike anything Phoebe had ever seen. *Paige is attracted to lots of guys, but there's never been anything like this. It isn't love. I don't think it's even lust. There's something strange about the whole thing. It's like she's under some kind of spell.*

Phoebe sighed and glanced at Paige. Her sister's face was glowing with an inner light, an excitement that Phoebe couldn't quite grasp. *Whatever is going on, I need to know what it is.*

"Here we are," Paige said, her voice breathy.

Phoebe stared at her, wishing she could get inside her sister's head. She followed Paige into the building and they joined a teeming mass of well-dressed people. She looked around. The elite of San Francisco were there, along with some outsiders and a few from across the Bay who seemed to be celebrating special occasions.

Such an event should have been exciting, but it wasn't. There was something hanging in the air that was almost tangible. Phoebe tried to grasp what it was, but it danced away from her elusively. Feeling frustrated, she followed Paige to their seats.

These aren't cheap seats, Phoebe realized as she looked around. *I wonder how Paige can afford to come night after night, and wearing a new dress each time. Oh well, that's none of my business. What is my business is why she keeps coming.*

With a start Phoebe realized that Paige was speaking. She tuned in just in time to hear, ". . . Dale has traveled the world playing. You'll love him."

"I'm sure I will," Phoebe said, not sure at all.

The lights flashed and all the patrons scurried to their seats. Phoebe watched them through narrowed eyes. They all seemed normal enough, but normal was a relative term, especially in the city. At least nothing seemed out of place.

I don't know what it is I'm looking for. It could be anything or anyone. There's just something wrong here, she thought.

At last the lights dimmed and stayed that way. Phoebe settled back into her seat, senses alert, determined to take in everything she could. Next to her, Paige's excitement was tangible, like electricity that Phoebe could actually feel.

The musicians took the stage, and even before Paige leaned over to point him out, Phoebe's eyes were immediately drawn to Dale. There was something special about him. She didn't have to hear him play to know that.

The music began but Phoebe barely heard it. She was focused more on her other senses, trying to determine exactly what it was that was amiss about the whole thing. She watched the musicians, the conductor, the people in the crowd.

She smelled the air, the perfume of the women, the cologne of the men, the age of the building. She felt the seat beneath her, the ground her feet rested on, the weight of the air on her skin.

And then, in a moment, all that changed. All her other senses faded away as her hearing came roaring to life. There was only one instrument singing and all the rest was silence, as though even the crowd held its breath.

"Dale," Phoebe whispered, watching him play. The music pierced her, taking her breath away. All of her senses were filled suddenly with him.

The music cut deep into her soul, until she

wanted to cry out in pain and ecstasy. She didn't know why, but she knew she would never forget it. There was something unnatural about the sound, and yet, she wished it was the only sound she could ever hear.

When the solo was finished she fell back into her seat, not even aware that she had nearly stood while he was playing. Her heart was pounding and she was sweating as though she had just run a marathon. There was also an emptiness in her, an unbearably lonely ache that she feared could only be filled by the sound of his flute.

At intermission she sat, still riveted, while Paige began to gush. Phoebe turned to her sister and saw a feverish light in Paige's eyes that she felt sure matched her own. In that moment she understood. Paige was under a spell, and now so was she. She didn't know if there was any way to free them from it. The worst part was, she wasn't sure she wanted to be free.

Before she could try to make sense of anything, the second half of the concert began. She waited with baited breath for Dale's next solo. When it came she cried out and grabbed Paige's arm. Paige was holding on to the note Dale had sent her a few nights ago at the symphony, and when Phoebe's hand touched it, a scream ripped through her mind, and her body convulsed with the pain of a vision stronger and more devastating than any she had ever felt.

She saw children, hundreds of children. Some lay dead, their bodies limp and lifeless. Others were dying, gasping their souls out with each breath. More stood, crying and afraid, watching the destruction. And she realized she wasn't just seeing the future, but also the past, and the *present*.

She gasped and looked at Dale. He was staring right at her, his eyes narrowed. *He knows that I know! He has killed them and he will continue to kill them. We have to stop him!*

And then she heard something, a voice speaking inside the notes the flute was playing. She looked around, but realized that no one else could hear it—they were all too enraptured. She turned back and heard the words, as clearly as if the flute were speaking. Its trembling voice whispered, "I am Death, and I will come for you next, now that you know."

Phoebe leaped to her feet, her hand still on Paige's arm, and dragged her sister with her up the aisle and out of the auditorium.

Paige fought her, but Phoebe's strength came from deep within and would not be denied. Once they reached the lobby, Phoebe walked them to a dark corner. Paige wrenched her arm away.

"What do you think you are doing?" she asked angrily.

"Getting us out of here," Phoebe lowered her voice to a whisper. "Paige, he's a demon."

Paige stood, still angry, her face incredulous, and Phoebe realized she could still hear the sounds of Dale's flute.

"Listen, Paige. Not just to the music, but to the words inside the notes. Listen hard," Phoebe urged.

Paige cocked her head to the side and closed her eyes. A look of horror slowly came over her face and Phoebe knew that she had heard. Dale's song was one of great beauty—and great evil. *The angel of death is supposed to be one of the most beautiful. Maybe his music is as well,* she thought.

"We've got to get out of here," Phoebe gasped. "We need to get back to the Manor."

"Done," Paige said.

They orbed out in a shimmer of light—

—and they orbed into chaos.

Children were everywhere, screaming and covered in blood. Phoebe began to shake in horror.

"Piper!" Paige screamed, but there was no answer.

Phoebe turned slowly, trying to take it all in. It was then that she saw Leo. He was sitting on the ground, cradling a child in his arms and weeping.

"Leo, what's wrong, what's happening?" Phoebe asked, dropping down beside him.

He looked up at her and she recoiled. Tears of blood were tracing their way down his cheeks. "I couldn't save him," he whispered.

Phoebe's heart broke for him.

"I saved the others, but I couldn't save him." He turned back to the boy's body as Phoebe struggled to find words. "How can I protect my own child if I can't protect these?" he asked.

Phoebe reached out and touched his shoulder. "Leo, it's okay. You can't save everyone. Every once in a while, we lose an Innocent. You've been there when it's happened to me. You have to let him go. And when the time comes, you will be able to protect your child, I'm sure of it."

"I'm not," he said.

"We are. And you won't be alone," Paige chimed in, kneeling next to her brother-in-law. "Right now, though, Leo, you have to let go and help us. You can't save this child, but there are others who need our help."

That seemed to reach him. He laid the child down gently on the ground and stood. His shirt was covered with blood and his face was strained.

"Now, what's going on here?" Phoebe asked.

Leo glanced around at the children. "They were dying. I healed them and brought them here for safety."

"What were they dying from?" Paige asked, her voice very quiet.

"Someone punched holes in their chests in an effort to pull out part of their essence."

"Not someone," Phoebe corrected. "It was Dale. He did this."

"Dale? But how?"

"I don't know," Phoebe admitted. "But I know that he did. I had a vision while I was at the concert. There's something in his music that spoke to me too."

"I hear he has that effect," Leo said grimly.

"No, I mean actually spoke to me, with words. He's evil and he's behind this."

"I'll go get Piper," Leo said. "After I bring this one to the hospital."

"No, I'll go," Paige said, her face twisted with pain. She orbed out without further discussion.

"She's not going to handle this well. She was under his spell and she's going to feel guilty," Phoebe guessed.

"Well, it wouldn't be a first," Leo said.

Phoebe laughed mirthlessly. "Truer words have never been spoken." She stared at all the hysterical children. "So what do we do with them now?"

Paige orbed into a storeroom at P3. She was crying and couldn't stop herself. *How could I be so blind? How could I not realize he was evil?* she wondered. Her knees buckled and she collapsed onto the ground, horror and guilt washing over her. *Kids are dying, and it's my fault!*

She knew she should get up, find Piper. Time was fleeting, but she couldn't make herself move. All she could do was sit and sob.

"Paige," she heard finally, "what are you doing here?"

She looked up and saw Piper standing in front of her.

"Oh, Piper, I've made such a mess of things!"

Piper knelt beside her. "What's wrong?"

All Paige could manage to say was, "We have to get back to the Manor." She reached out to take Piper's hand to orb them both home.

Nothing.

Focus, Paige, you can do this. You just have to relax and focus.

They began to orb, but stopped.

"Paige, what's wrong?" Piper asked again, a hard edge to her voice.

"Everything."

Paige closed her eyes, thought about home. There was a slight rush and then the sound of crying children. She opened her eyes. *Home.*

She collapsed onto the floor.

Piper looked around in amazement. "What on earth is going on here?"

Phoebe, sitting on the couch, stared at her. She shrugged, opened her mouth, and then closed it again as a swarm of children launched themselves at Piper.

"Piper, Piper," the children sniffled as many hands grabbed at her legs.

"Whoa, whoa. Hold it! Why are these kids here and why are they all bloody? Why is Leo crying? Why has Paige collapsed on the floor?"

No one answered her. She turned to Phoebe with more unasked questions.

"I'm not sure I can explain, but I'll try," Phoebe said, taking a deep breath. "We were at the concert and I had a vision. I saw children dying and Dale had something to do with it. It was like I saw him for what he was. So did Paige. Leo's been orbing around, healing children who have had their life force sucked from them. All the children had musical talent and some of them we've come to know pretty well."

Piper looked around in horror. "So what exactly is it that Dale wants?" she asked.

"Perhaps I can answer that," a deep voice said behind her.

Chapter
10

Piper twisted around to see Dale Allen standing in the hallway. She brought her hands up to freeze him, but before she could, he disappeared.

"Where did he go?" she yelled.

"Ssh, do you hear that?" Paige said, looking up past Piper to the door.

A sweet, haunting tune was coming from the kitchen. Everyone fell quiet, listening.

"No!" Phoebe shouted, jumping to her feet. "Whatever you do, don't listen." She ran into the other room.

"Why can't we listen?" Piper asked. Then the music struck her, a calming force in the chaos of all the children who had been surrounding her for days. It was a melody that was over-powering and it brought tears to her eyes.

Phoebe! Phoebe's going to stop the music, Piper thought. She started to chase after Phoebe, but stopped, filled with the haunting refrain. *He has to finish his song.* She closed her eyes and swayed gently.

"Flute!" Paige shouted from behind her.

The music stopped suddenly, and crying out, Piper opened her eyes. She turned just in time to see Paige orbing out, Dale's flute in her hand. "No!" Piper cried. She turned back toward Dale, feeling lost and confused.

"That's my cue," he said with a dip of his head before he, too, disappeared.

"He's gone," Piper sobbed, putting her head in her hands.

Into the silence a tiny voice quavered, "I want to go home."

"Well, that was a stunning failure," Phoebe noted dryly.

"I'm not sure what just happened," Piper said, sitting down on the couch.

"Why do I always end up with demons?" Paige complained.

"It's the Halliwell curse," Piper told her.

"Or, it could be that evil can be very attractive, especially when it wants to be," Phoebe interjected.

"Still, Dale Allen, Allen O'Dale, how could I be so stupid?" Paige asked glumly.

"I don't get it," Phoebe said.

"Allen O'Dale is an old-time minstrel name, a medieval musician."

"Oh. How did you know that?" Phoebe asked, wrinkling her brow.

"Everyone knows that," Paige said, throwing her hands up. Seeing the blank faces of her sisters, she added, "Okay, maybe not everyone. I was big into fairy tales as a kid."

Piper chimed in. "I still don't get what he did to me."

"The music—he was enchanting you with it," Paige said.

"Huh. What did you do with the flute?" Piper asked.

"I tossed it into a volcano," Paige answered.

"Shame. That was a beautiful flute," Piper quipped.

Phoebe whapped Piper on the arm.

"Ow! Sorry, sheesh."

Leo orbed in looking worried. "How are the kids?" he asked, glancing around.

"Asleep," Phoebe answered. "Their parents aren't going to forgive us for keeping them overnight."

"We don't have a lot of choice. This is the only place they're even remotely safe."

"So, did you find out anything?" Piper asked, her tone biting.

"As a matter of fact, I did," he said.

"So spill. What are we dealing with?"

"You know the story of the Pied Piper?" Leo asked.

"Isn't that the guy who played his pipe and

caused all the children to follow him out of town?" Phoebe asked.

"Yeah, and they, like, disappeared through a hole or vortex or something and were never seen again," Paige contributed.

"All but one, who fell behind," Leo said.

"Because he had a crippled foot," Piper said slowly, her voice distant.

"You know the story?"

Piper wrinkled her nose. "No, let's just say it's a lucky guess."

"What? What is it?" Leo asked.

"I think he paid me a visit."

"The piper?" Paige asked.

"No, the boy with the crippled foot. Well, man, now."

"That would mean he'd have to be a couple hundred years old," Leo said.

"You see, I was afraid you were going to say something like that," Piper said.

It didn't take Leo long to find the old man. He was standing right on the doorstep of the Manor, looking for all the world like he had been waiting for someone to open the door and invite him in.

Leo stepped aside to let the man by, and Piper stood to confront him.

"Who are you?" she asked.

"I am the last, but then, you already know that."

"The last? The last what? What do you mean?"

Piper demanded, her temper flaring. "I know you did this—whatever it is—to me. Why?"

"So many questions," he said with a smile. "I will answer what I can in the time we have left for such things."

"Great, that sounds nice and ominous," Paige said.

"Your affections are misplaced," the old man said to Paige.

"You mean Dale? Yeah, thanks. I kind of figured that out for myself already."

"Look, whatever your name is, we need answers," Phoebe said.

"I am he of the crippled foot, the child left behind, forgotten and unseen. I am the last descendant of my people, the only one, and when I am gone they will have gone."

"Okay, so, you're the kid in the Pied Piper story."

He dipped his head in acknowledgment.

"That would make you—"

"*Very* old," he said. "I have kept myself alive only by the use of certain spells. I have searched for the piper ever since, to stop him from taking other children."

"What does he do with them?" Paige asked.

The old man sighed heavily. "I think you have seen some of his work already, on the children that could not escape him."

"We have," Leo answered grimly.

"I put a spell on Piper, so the children would

come to her instead of the piper. I needed a witch in order for the spell to work. You have a natural aura of light; children can sense it and would be more likely to gravitate to you anyway. When the piper comes to a town, his music draws children to him. In the old days, when villages were small, he called all children. Now he calls only those with musical talent of their own."

The old man stopped, drawing in a long breath. He continued, "The piper needs their music, their inspiration and creative spark, to survive. He steals it from them and feeds himself. His talent grows while those he robs die without reaching their potential or enriching the world."

"And you fixed it so that instead of being drawn to him, they would be drawn to me?" Piper asked, aghast.

"Yes," the old man said. "I knew you could protect them. Alas, not all of the children were able to come to you. Their guardians kept watch on them so they could not stray from home."

"And those that made it here—I took them home anyway," Piper realized.

"It's okay, honey, you had no way of knowing," Leo said, putting a hand on her shoulder.

"And then I led Dale right to them," Paige said bitterly.

"You couldn't have known either, sweetie," Phoebe said.

"The important thing is, now that we know what we're dealing with, we can do something about it," Leo reminded them.

"We need to regroup, focus," Phoebe said.

"I thought that's what we were doing," Paige said, sarcasm dripping from her voice.

"Okay, let's not fight among ourselves," Leo said soothingly.

"Hah! Easy enough for you to say," Piper replied.

The old man raised his hands. "Please, you must all work together. He must be stopped before more children are lost."

"He's right," Paige said, her voice sounding far off. A smile spread across her face. "And I know just the potion to take care of our little problem."

"Then let's get on it," Piper said.

Driving home from work, Darryl listened to his cell phone messages. When he heard Piper's voice he thought about pushing delete without listening to it. He didn't, though. Once the message had finished, he turned his car and headed straight for the Manor.

"I know I'm going to regret this," he muttered.

Traffic was snarled and it took him longer than he liked. "Come on, come on," he called to the cars ahead of him, wishing he was a witch and could magically move them.

At last he pulled up outside the Manor and raced inside with his gun drawn.

"Darryl, you're here. Great," said Piper.

"Where is he?"

"Not here, thank goodness, we're not ready for him."

"Well, isn't that just too bad," a man said behind him.

As Darryl turned, the gun was knocked from his hand. It went flying and skidded underneath the sofa. Another punch sent Darryl to the ground, and everything went black.

When he woke up, children were screaming and jumping on top of him. "What is going on?" he shouted as one child wrapped a hand around his belt. The kids pulled at him, but they were above him, hovering in midair. It was like they were being pulled toward something—*like that thing at the end of Poltergeist that sucked everything in the room, including the kids, toward it,* he realized with a shudder. *Man, I hated that movie.*

"Hold on, kids. I won't let go," he said, wrapping his hand under the bottom of the couch to anchor himself.

Chapter

11

Phoebe and Dale had battled their way into the dining room before Dale hit her hard, sending her flying back into the living room.

Paige stood before him, trembling, but strong. "It's over, Dale, give up."

"Afraid I can't do that."

"What are you going to do without your flute?" Paige taunted.

He laughed; it was a deep, booming sound. "Dear Paige, surely you don't think I've used that instrument my whole life, do you?"

From his pocket he pulled a small clay pipe, and before she could do anything he raised it to his lips.

"Pipe!" she called, extending her hand.

Nothing happened. "Pipe!" she shouted.

He lifted his right eyebrow and she could tell

he was smiling at her even though the instrument blocked her view of his lips.

The pipe is insulated from my magic, she realized.

She watched helplessly as Dale began to play and a portal flared into life on the far side of the dining room. It shimmered with all the colors of the rainbow and music swelled from it. The children begin to scream, but Paige kept her eyes fixed on Dale.

Dale put his pipe down. "The portal pulls at them, and it will draw them through. You can come with us," he said.

"You're going to murder all these children," she accused.

"Actually, I'm going to make them immortal. Their music—their inspiration—will live on in me forever. I give that music a voice. Most of these kids will never accomplish anything grander than playing a recital for a handful of parents. This way, they can all be great."

"But they have to die for it!" Paige shouted. Anger and the bitter feeling of betrayal gripped her. She could feel the vial containing the vanquishing potion in the palm of her hand, smooth and cold. There was passion in the potion that she had mixed so carefully in the fit of inspiration inspired by Dale's music. There was no life in the potion, though, only death. If she threw it, she would be killing Dale and his music and everything they meant to her.

Dale's eyes bored into her own. "Those children will grow up and die anyway, without fame, without reaching their potential. Now they have a chance to be part of something bigger, to create music that will outlive them."

"That's not right. Everyone deserves a chance to achieve their own potential, find their own immortality," Paige said.

"Some, yes, but only those who truly understand the gift they have been given and have the vision to use it well. Unfortunately, there are very few Beethovens, but a myriad of church pianists who lack the courage to really challenge themselves."

"But it's not for you to choose, not for you to know who will become great and who will not," Paige argued.

"Ah, there is where you are wrong. I do know, I can sense it. There's a child right now in this house who has the skill to be one of the greatest ever, but he has no love for the music and will not pursue it."

"Then that's his right, his choice, and you're not going to take that away from him." Paige knew it was true, but she could barely grasp it. All she could truly believe was that Dale was standing before her and all she could truly feel was his power over her.

"My dear Paige, you can't stop me," he said condescendingly.

"Maybe she can't, but together we can," Phoebe said from the doorway.

Shaken, Paige blinked and risked a glance sideways. She saw Phoebe standing beside Piper, steel in their eyes.

"The Charmed Ones. You know, I couldn't believe my fortune. The power that I could draw from you would keep me alive for centuries."

"But we're not musical," Piper said.

"No, but you're magical, and that has its own rewards."

Paige clutched the potion in her hand, willing herself to throw it at him, knowing that she should.

Piper raised her hands and tried to freeze him, to no effect. Phoebe charged at him, but he tossed her aside like a rag doll.

My sisters cannot help me. Only I can do this. He cannot be defeated by force or by magic, but only by inspiration. Inspiration is what I hold in my hand, and it can kill him, Paige thought.

"Come with me," Dale urged her.

"I can't," she whispered, shaking from head to toe.

"You heard the music; you understand."

"I do," she admitted.

"Then come with me."

Tears filled her eyes. "No, Dale. I'm not going anywhere with you."

Paige was surprised to see Dale's face turn dark with disappointment. "All right, but the children *are* coming with me." He turned toward the portal. "I meant what I said, Paige," he told her, standing with one foot in the portal. "I really do want to be your friend." His face was earnest, his eyes entreating, and his smile enticing.

Paige shook her head slowly, freeing herself once and for all from his influence. "Sorry, but I'm not friends with demons," she said. Taking a deep breath, she threw the vial at him.

The glass shattered, and the liquid splashed against him. His eyes widened in realization and met Paige's. She could see that Dale knew he was going to die, and she wanted to look away, but she couldn't, pinned by his accusing stare.

The sound of thousands of musical instruments filled the air. Paige clapped her hands over her ears to block the deafening symphony, which she realized was made from all the music Dale had stolen over the centuries. *All the music he's taken from other people*. It poured out of him, a last magnificent piece more terrible and beautiful than anything he had ever played. Paige fell to her knees before it, her heart breaking. At last the music came to a mighty crescendo and Dale exploded in a wave of light so brilliant she had to look away.

In a moment the music was gone and Paige's attention was drawn to a new sound. With the music gone, she could hear Darryl shouting and kids screaming in the living room. She ran toward the noise and saw Darryl, lying flat on his back in the middle of the living-room floor, with kids hanging on him.

"What the . . . ?" she said, bewildered.

"We're being pulled toward the portal!" Mark shouted.

Paige looked again and realized that the kids hanging off Darryl's arms, legs, and even the one with a fist wrapped around Darryl's belt, were all being pulled toward the dining room.

"Help! Please!" Darryl shouted.

"Help us!" Paige pleaded, turning to the old man. He remained on the floor, where he had been struck down. He struggled to a sitting position, his head bleeding from where Dale had wounded him.

"I'm sorry, truly I am," he said, staggering to his feet.

He hobbled into the dining room and stood for a moment, staring at the portal. He moved toward it and Paige wondered if he could close it.

"All my life I've wondered what was on the other side. I have to know," he whispered. Turning, he gave her a sad, sweet smile. "Maybe they are waiting for me."

He pulled a flute out of his pocket and tossed it toward the dining room. Then he stepped inside the portal and vanished from sight.

"No!" Piper shouted, but it was too late.

Paige turned and watched the flute tumbling end over end through the air toward Darryl

and the children. *I have to get it!* she thought
frantically.

Before she could move, though, Mark grabbed
the flute out of midair. With his legs still
wrapped around Darryl's, he brought the flute to
his lips and began to play. The music seemed to
spiral directly toward the portal. The portal pul-
sated once and then resumed its shape.

"Keep playing, Mark!" Piper shouted.

A girl lost her hold on Darryl and, screaming,
went hurtling toward the portal. Phoebe grabbed
her as she whizzed by, stopping her progress.

"I've got you, just hold on," Phoebe shouted,
face twisting in pain.

Mark continued playing, closing his eyes. The
music poured forth, hauntingly beautiful. Paige
stared at the portal, willing it to close, desperately hoping that Mark could do it.

An older boy flew by and Paige tackled him
to the ground. She tried to orb, but only shimmered briefly in place.

"The pull on the child must be too great for
you to break him free from it," Piper called. "Just
stay down."

Paige nodded, covering the child with as
much of her body as she could.

It's working! Piper realized.

But suddenly the music stopped. Piper turned
wildly toward Mark. "Keep playing!" she begged.

"I can't!" he cried.

Piper could see the fear in his face. His legs were losing their hold on Darryl.

"Yes, you can, Mark. I believe in you. Reach inside and use your passion. Whatever it is you love, whatever it is you want to be, express that, the pipe is your voice, you have to speak the words."

Mark brought the pipe back to his lips and began to play again. The music came out strong, filling the room. *There's power in it,* Piper realized with wonder. *And something . . .*

A shout from Phoebe caused Piper to turn back to the portal. As she watched, it began to shrink slowly, though its pull was still strong. She turned to offer Mark encouragement, but the words died on her lips. He was hovering in midair, his legs no longer wrapped around Darryl. His eyes were wide open and there was a look of purpose on his face. It was then that she heard the words in the music. *Close forever and leave us alone.*

The portal vanished and all around Piper heard the sound of children falling to the floor. Except for Mark, who remained, hovering for a moment in midair before coming down lightly on his feet as he played the last note.

He put the pipe down and looked at Piper. She dropped to her knees and he ran into her arms, hugging her fiercely. "Mark, what is it you want to be?" she asked softly, holding the boy close.

His voice was barely a whisper as he answered, "A witch."

With Leo's help, Darryl returned all of the children to their homes except for Mark. The sisters sat around Mark in the living room, talking quietly with him.

When Leo returned, he nodded to Piper to let her know that everything was okay, and then sat down on the couch between Mark and Paige. "You okay there, big guy?" he asked.

Mark nodded. "Yes. I never knew I could do that."

"You had some suspicions, though?" Piper asked.

"Well, my mom is a witch."

The doorbell rang. Leo rose to get it, and returned a moment later with a woman in tow.

"Mark!" she cried, falling to her knees and wrapping her arms around her son.

"How did you find his mother?" Piper asked.

"Remember when I said I had a good excuse, and you didn't want to hear it?" Leo told her.

"Yeah," Piper said, with the feeling that her statement was about to come back and bite her.

"I was watching over a witch who has only recently discovered her powers," Leo said. "This is Sandra."

"You mean . . ."

"I didn't realize Mark knew," Sandra said. "I was hoping he wouldn't discover his own powers until he was older. I wanted him to have a normal life, pursue music or something else," Sandra said.

Remembering the letter she had read at work, Phoebe suddenly took a step forward. "You wouldn't by any chance be Mother of Talented Son?"

"Yes, I'm the one who wrote to you," Sandra admitted shyly.

"Then I have an answer for you," Phoebe said. "I can tell you care deeply for your son. Let your son pursue what he loves, not what you think he should love."

"That's good advice," Sandra admitted, tears sparkling in her eyes.

"I want to visit Piper sometimes," Mark said.

"If it's okay with Piper, it's okay with me," Sandra answered, hugging her son close.

Piper smiled. "I would like that."

Sandra ruffled her son's hair. "Come on, Mark. Let's go home. You, Dad, and I have some things to discuss." Turning to Piper she said, "Thank you, for everything."

"You're welcome," Piper said. "And, thank *you*, Mark."

The little boy only smiled.

After Sandra and Mark left, Piper turned to Leo.

"Leo, you know that thing I didn't want to talk about?" Piper asked.

"Having kids?"

"Yeah, that."

"Listen, Piper. You've had a bad few days. I promise you it wouldn't be like that. First off, we're not talking about several kids, we're talking about one—two, max. And we would be the ones raising them, the way we thought they should be raised. I know you saw some real brats, but our child wouldn't be like that."

"You feel pretty strongly about this, don't you?" Piper asked.

"I do," Leo said, his eyes shining.

"Well, that's good, because so do I. These last few days have shown me the worst parts of being a mom. But there were some really good things about it, too. I think I'm ready."

"Ready to talk about it?" Leo asked.

She smiled and leaned forward. Putting her arms around his neck, she leaned her face toward his. "More like ready to stop *talking* about it." She kissed him slowly, suggestively.

When she pulled away she saw tears dancing in his eyes. "You mean . . . ?" he asked, his voice unsure.

"Yes, I do. Want to try and make a baby?"

The doorbell rang and when no one seemed to be around to get it, Leo broke his embrace with Piper and headed for the door. He came back a moment later with a baby in his arms.

"Wow, you work fast," Piper said, a little off balance.

Leo laughed. "Look who's back!" he said with a smile.

"Oh no," Piper said, backing away as she recognized Gracie. "Where did she come from?"

"Her brother must be around here somewhere," Leo said.

"Hello!" a little voice chirped, as though on cue, poking his head out from behind Leo.

Piper rolled her eyes. "Keep that baby away from me."

"Come on, Piper. You want to have one, you're going to have to get used to some little inconveniences."

The baby turned its head slightly and Leo shouted. "She bit me! Get her off."

"How about those little inconveniences, Leo? Feel good now?" Piper asked. She started laughing and turned to embrace Phoebe and Paige, who'd both come downstairs. They were both howling with laughter.

"This isn't funny," Leo called. "I need help."

As they laughed, the sisters held on to one another so they wouldn't fall down.

This is going to be fun, Piper thought.

About the Author

Debbie Viguié has been writing since she was ten. She holds a degree in English with a creative writing emphasis from UC Davis. She is the author of *Midnight Pearls* and *Scarlet Moon* and the coauthor of the Wicked series. When she's not writing, Debbie likes to spend her time traveling with her husband and visiting with friends.

MYSTIC KNOLL

All vanquishing and no time for play makes for tired, grumpy Charmed Ones. Paige decides that what they need is a family getaway, but where to go? She'd love to explore her witch heritage in Salem, but that doesn't sound very relaxing to Phoebe and Piper, who'd rather spend a week on a quiet beach, soaking up the sun. Sensing a sibling showdown, Leo points out that they can do both. They'll spend a day or two in Salem, then the rest of the time on the beautiful Massachusetts coast.

Late flights and wrong directions conspire to sidetrack the travelers, and they find themselves hungry and exhausted and nowhere near Salem. Luckily they happen upon a bed-and-breakfast run by a crotchety old woman and her strange, shy granddaughter. They're not your typical innkeepers—and soon Piper, Phoebe, and Paige find that nothing in this small town is typical. It's all a little . . . well . . . *mystical*. Maybe those directions weren't wrong after all—looks like a working vacation for the Charmed Ones!

"We all need to believe that magic exists."

–Phoebe Halliwell, "Trial by Magic"

When Phoebe Halliwell returned to San Francisco to live with her older sisters, Prue and Piper, in Halliwell Manor, she had no idea the turn her life—*all* their lives—would take. Because when Phoebe found the Book of Shadows in the Manor's attic, she learned that she and her sisters were the Charmed Ones, the most powerful witches of all time. Battling demons, warlocks, and other powerful forces of black magic, Piper and Phoebe lost Prue but discovered their long-lost half-Whitelighter, half-witch sister, Paige Matthews. The Power of Three was reborn.

Look out for other new Charmed novels!

Published by Simon & Schuster

™ & © 2004 Spelling Television Inc. All Rights Reserved.

"We're the protectors of the innocent.
We're known as the Charmed Ones."

–Phoebe Halliwell, "Something Wicca This Way Comes"

Go behind the scenes of television's sexiest supernatural thriller with *The Book of Three*, the *only* fully authorized companion to the witty, witchy world of *Charmed*!

Published by Simon & Schuster